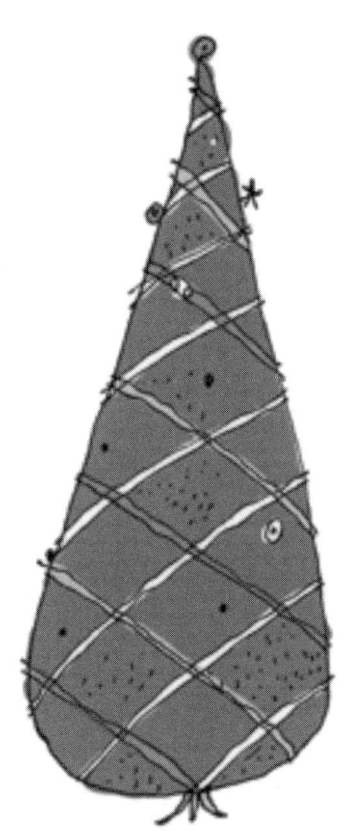

A VERY RUSSIAN CHRISTMAS

The Greatest Russian Holiday Stories of All Time

NEW VESSEL PRESS
NEW YORK

www.newvesselpress.com

Cover design: Liana Finck
Book design: Beth Steidle

Library of Congress Cataloging-in-Publication Data
Various
The Greatest Russian Christmas Stories of All Time / various authors.
p. cm.
ISBN 978-1-939931-43-6
Library of Congress Control Number 2016903935
I. Russia – Fiction

TABLE OF CONTENTS

A VERY RUSSIAN CHRISTMAS

THE NEW YEAR'S TREE

Mikhail Zoshchenko

(In the Soviet Union, it was forbidden to celebrate Christmas. In order to keep the much beloved custom of the Christmas Tree—and oneself—alive, the New Year's tree was born.)

This year I turned forty, friends. Turns out, I've seen forty New Year's trees. That's a lot!

I guess the first three years of life I didn't really know what a New Year's tree was. I guess Mama took me by the hand. And I guess, with my little black eyes I looked with disinterest at the decorated tree.

But, children, when the age of five struck, I could understood perfectly what a New Year's tree was. And I couldn't wait for this joyous holiday to come around.

My big sister was seven at the time. And she was an exceptionally bright little girl. She said to me one day, "Minka, Mama's in the kitchen. Let's go into the room where the tree is and take a look at what's going on there."

And so my sister, Lyolya, and I went into the room. And what did we see: a very beautiful New Year's tree. And underneath the tree were presents. And beads, bunting, lanterns, acorns, pastilles, and Crimean apples.

My sister, Lyolya, said, "We won't peek at the presents. Instead, better yet let's each eat one little pastille." And so she walked up to the tree and in an instant she gulped down a pastille that was hanging on a string.

I said, "Lyolya, if you ate a pastille, then I want to eat something." And I walked right up to the New Year's tree and took a nibble from an apple.

Lyolya said, "Minka, if you took a nibble from the apple, then I'm going to eat a second pastille and in addition, I'll take this piece of candy for myself."

Now, Lyolya was tall, a very long-limbed, gawky girl. And she could reach up high. She stood on her tippy toes and with her big mouth began to eat a second pastille. And I was surprisingly short. I could barely reach anything, except for the one apple which hung low.

"Lyolisha, if you ate a second pastille, then I'll take another bite from the apple." And I took the apple in my hands one more time and nibbled.

Lyolya said, "If you took another bite from the apple, then I won't stand on ceremony anymore and I'm going to eat a third pastille and in addition I'm going to take this bonbon cracker as a souvenir." I almost screamed. Because she could reach everything, and I couldn't.

I said to her, "Well, Lyolisha, I'll bring a chair up to the tree and I'll grab something for myself, something besides an apple."

And so with my skinny little arms I began to drag a chair over to the tree. But the chair fell on me. I wanted to pick it up. But it fell again. And right on the presents.

Lyolya said, "Minka, looks like you broke the puppet. That's right. You broke the porcelain arm off of the puppet."

Just then we heard Mama's footsteps and Lyolya and I ran into the other room.

Lyolya said, "Now, Minka, I can't guarantee that Mama won't wallop you."

I wanted to scream but at that moment guests arrived. A bunch of kids with their parents. Our mom lit all the candles on the tree, opened the door and said:

"Everybody come in."

And all the kids walked into the room where the New Year's tree was standing.

Our mama said, "And now let every child come to me, and I will give each one a toy and a treat."

And so the kids started going up to our mom. And she gave each one a toy. Then she took an apple, a pastille, and a candy from the tree and gave those to the children, too. And all the kids were very happy. Then Mama grabbed the apple I'd taken a bite out of and she said, "Lyolya and Minka, come here right now. Which one of you took a nibble from the apple?"

Lyolya said, "That's Minka's work."

I grabbed Lyolya by her little braid and said, "Lyolya showed me the ropes."

Mama said, "I'm putting Lyolya in the corner, nose first. As for you, however, I was going to give you a steamboat. But now I'm going to give the steamboat to that little boy I wanted to give the half-nibbled apple to."

And she took the steamboat and gave it to a four-year-old boy. And that boy began playing with it in an instant. And I got angry at the little boy and hit him in the arm with the toy. And he began to howl so awfully that his own mother took him by the hand and said, "From this day on I will not make another visit here with my boy."

And I said, "You can leave and I'll keep the steamboat."

And the other mother was surprised at my words and said: "Your son, no doubt, will be a brigand." And then my mother took me by the hand and said to that mother:

"Don't dare speak about my son that way. You better leave now with your golden boy and never, ever return to our home." And that other mother said:

"I'll do just that. Here, one arrives a guest and leaves distressed." And then another, a third mother, said:

"I'm going as well. My little girl doesn't deserve to be given a puppet with a chipped arm."

And my sister Lyolya shouted, "You can go too, with your golden girl! And I'll keep the puppet with the broken arm."

And then I, sitting on my mother's lap, shouted, "And anyway everybody can leave, and we'll keep all the toys." And all the guests began leaving. And our mother was surprised that we were left alone. But suddenly our papa came into the room.

He said, "Such an upbringing will ruin my children. I don't want them to fight, argue with, or kick out our guests. They'll have a difficult time in this world, and they'll die alone." And Papa walked up to the New Year's tree and snuffed out all the lights. And then he said:

"Get in bed this instant. Tomorrow I'll give the presents to the guests." And so, my friends, thirty-five years have gone by since then and I still remember that tree, even now. And for the past thirty-five years, children, I've never once eaten somebody else's apple and never hit somebody who was weaker than me. And the doctors tell me that's why I'm happy and good-hearted, relatively speaking.

1939

THE BOYS

Anton Chekhov

"VOLODIA is here!" cried someone in the courtyard.

"Volodichka is here!" shrieked Natalia, rushing into the dining room.

The whole family ran to the window, for they had been expecting their Volodia for hours. At the front porch stood a wide posting sleigh with its troika of white horses wreathed in dense clouds of steam. The sleigh was empty because Volodia was already standing in the front entry untying his hood with red, frostbitten fingers. His schoolboy's uniform, his overcoat, his cap, his galoshes, and the hair on his temples were all silvery with frost, and from his head to his feet he exhaled such a wholesome atmosphere of cold that one shivered to be near him. His mother and aunt rushed to kiss and embrace him. Natalia fell down at his feet and began pulling off his galoshes. His sisters shrieked, doors creaked and banged on every side, and his father came running into the hall in his shirt-sleeves waving a pair of scissors and crying in alarm:

"Is anything the matter? We expected you yesterday. Did you have a good journey? For heaven's sake, give him a chance to kiss his own father!"

"Bow, wow, wow!" barked the great black dog, Milord, in a deep voice, banging the walls and furniture with his tail.

All these noises went to make up one great, joyous clamor that lasted several minutes. When the first burst of joy had subsided the family noticed that, beside Volodia, there was still another small person in the hall. He was wrapped in scarfs and shawls and hoods and was standing motionless in the shadow cast by a huge fox-skin coat.

"Volodia, who is that?" whispered Volodia's mother.

"Good gracious!" Volodia exclaimed, recollecting himself. "Let me present my friend Chechevitsyn. I have brought him from school to stay with us."

"We are delighted to see you! Make yourself at home!" cried the father gaily. "Excuse my not having a coat on! Allow me!—Natalia, help Mr. Cherepitsyn to take off his things! For heaven's sake, take that dog away! This noise is too awful!"

A few minutes later Volodia and his friend were sitting in the dining room drinking tea, dazed by their noisy reception and still rosy with cold. The wintry rays of the sun, piercing the frost and snow on the windowpanes, trembled over the samovar and bathed themselves in the rinse basin. The room was warm, and the boys felt heat and cold jostling one another in their bodies, neither wanting to concede its place to the other.

"Well, Christmas will soon be here!" cried Volodia's father, rolling a cigarette. "Has it seemed long since your mother cried as she saw you off last summer? Time flies, my son! Old age comes before one has time to heave a sigh. Mr. Chibisoff, do help yourself! We don't stand on ceremony here!"

Volodia's three sisters, Katia, Sonia, and Masha, the oldest of whom was eleven, sat around the table with their eyes fixed on their new acquaintance. Chechevitsyn was the same age and size as Volodia, but he was neither plump nor fair like him. He was swarthy and thin and his face was covered with freckles. His hair was bristly, his eyes were small, and his lips were thick; in a word, he was very plain, and, had it not been for his schoolboy's uniform, he might have been taken for the son of a cook. He was taciturn and morose, and he never once smiled. The girls immediately decided that he must be a very clever and learned person. He seemed to be meditating something, and was so busy with his own thoughts that he started if he were asked a question, and asked to have it repeated.

The girls noticed that Volodia, who was generally so talkative and gay, seldom spoke now and never smiled and on the whole did not seem glad to be at home. He only addressed his sisters once during dinner and then his remark was strange. He pointed to the samovar and said:

"In California they drink gin instead of tea."

He, too, seemed to be busy with thoughts of his own, and, to judge from the glances that the two boys occasionally exchanged, their thoughts were identical.

After tea the whole family went into the nursery, and Papa and the girls sat down at the table and took up some work which they had been doing when they were interrupted by the boys' arrival. They were making decorations out of colored paper for the Christmas tree. It was a thrilling and noisy occupation. Each new flower was greeted by the girls with shrieks of ecstasy, of terror almost, as if it had dropped from the sky. Papa, too, was in raptures, but every now and then he would throw down the scissors, exclaiming angrily that they were blunt. Mama came running into the nursery with an anxious face and asked:

"Who has taken my scissors? Have you taken my scissors again, Ivan?"

"Good heavens, won't she even let me have a pair of scissors?" answered Papa in a tearful voice, throwing himself back in his chair with the air of a much-abused man. But the next moment he was in raptures again.

On former holidays Volodia had always helped with the preparations for the Christmas tree, and had run out into the yard to watch the coachman and the shepherd heaping up a mound of snow, but this time neither he nor Chechevitsyn took any notice of the colored paper, nor did they once visit the stables. They sat by a window whispering together, and then opened an atlas and fell to studying it.

"First, we must go to Perm," whispered Chechevitsyn. "Then to Tyumen, then to Tomsk, and then—then to Kamchatka. From there the Eskimos will take us across the Behring Strait in their canoes, and then—we shall be in America! There are a great many wild animals there."

"Where is California?" asked Volodia.

"California is farther down. If we can get to America, California will be around the corner. We can make our living by hunting and highway robbery."

All day Chechevitsyn avoided the girls and, if he met them, looked at them askance. After tea in the evening he was left alone with them for five minutes. To remain silent would have been awkward, so he coughed sternly, rubbed the back of his right hand with the palm of his left, looked severely at Katia, and asked:

"Have you read Mayne Reid?"

"No, I haven't … but tell me, can you skate?"

Chechevitsyn became lost in thought once more and did not answer her question. He only blew out his cheeks and heaved a sigh as if he were very hot. Once more he raised his eyes to Katia's face and said:

"When a herd of buffalo gallop across the pampas the whole earth trembles and the frightened mustangs kick and neigh."

Chechevitsyn smiled wistfully and added:

"And Indians attack trains, too. But worst of all are the mosquitoes and the termites."

"What are those?"

"Termites look something like ants, only they have wings. They bite dreadfully. Do you know who I am?"

"You are Mr. Chechevitsyn!"

"No, I am Montehomo, the Hawk's Claw, Chief of the Ever Victorious Hawkeye."

Masha, the youngest of the girls, looked first at him and then out of the window into the garden, where night was already falling, and said doubtfully:

"We had something called *chechevitsa* for supper last night."[1] The absolutely unintelligible sayings of Chechevitsin, his continual whispered conversations with Volodia, and the fact that Volodia never played now and was always absorbed in thought—all this seemed to the girls to be both mysterious and strange. Katia and Sonia, the two oldest ones, began to spy on the boys, and when Volodia and his friend went to bed that evening, they crept to the door of their room and listened to the conversation inside. Oh! What did they hear? The boys were planning to run away to America in search of gold! They were all prepared for the journey and had a pistol ready, two knives, some bread crusts, a magnifying glass for lighting fires, a compass, and four rubles. The girls discovered that the boys would have to walk several thousand miles, fight-

---

1. In Russian, chechevitsa means lentils, thus making a pun out of the young protagonist's odd name.

ing on the way with savages and tigers, and that they would then find gold and ivory, and slay their enemies. Next, they would turn pirates, drink gin, and at last marry beautiful wives and settle down to cultivate a plantation. Volodia and Chechevitsyn both talked at once and kept interrupting one another from excitement. Chechevitsyn named himself "Montehomo, the Hawk's Claw," and he called Volodia "my Paleface Brother."

"Be sure you don't tell Mama!" said Katia to Sonia as they went back to bed. "Volodia will bring us gold and ivory from America, but if you tell Mama she won't let him go!"

Chechevitsyn spent the day before Christmas Eve studying a map of Asia and taking notes, while Volodia roamed about the house refusing all food, his face looking tired and puffy as if it had been stung by a bee. He stopped more than once in front of the icon in the nursery and crossed himself saying:

"O Lord, forgive me, miserable sinner! O Lord, help my poor, unfortunate mother!"

Toward evening he burst into tears. When he said good night he kissed his father and mother and sisters over and over again. Katia and Sonia realized the significance of his actions, but Masha, the youngest, understood nothing at all. Only when her eye fell upon Chechevitsyn did she grow pensive and say with a sigh:

"Nurse says that when Lent comes we must eat peas and chechevitsa."

Early on Christmas Eve Katia and Sonia slipped quietly out of bed and went to the boys' room to see them run away to America. They crept up to their door.

"So you won't go?" asked Chechevitsyn angrily. "Tell me, you won't go?"

"Oh, dear!" wailed Volodia, weeping softly. "How can I go? I'm so sorry for Mama!"

"Paleface Brother, I beg you to go! You promised me yourself that you would. You told me yourself how nice it would be. Now, when everything is ready, you are afraid!"

"I … I'm not afraid. I … I'm sorry for Mama."

"Tell me, are you going or not?"

"I'm going, only … only wait a bit, I want to stay at home a little while longer!"

"If that's the case, I'll go alone!" Chechevitsyn said with decision. "I can get along perfectly well without you. I want to hunt and fight tigers! If you won't go, give me my pistol!"

Volodia began to cry so bitterly that his sisters could not endure the sound and began weeping softly themselves. Silence fell.

"Then you won't go?" demanded Chechevitsyn again.

"I … I'll go."

"Then get dressed!"

And to keep up Volodia's courage, Chechevitsyn began singing the praises of America. He roared like a tiger, he whistled like a steamboat, he scolded, and promised to give Volodia all the ivory and gold they might find.

The thin, dark boy with his bristling hair and his freckles seemed to the girls to be a strange and wonderful person. He was a hero to them, a man without fear, who could roar so well that, through the closed door, one might really mistake him for a tiger or a lion.

When the girls were dressing in their own room, Katia exclaimed with tears in her eyes:

"Oh, I'm so frightened!"

All was quiet until the family sat down to dinner at two o'clock, and then it suddenly appeared that the boys were not in the house. Inquiries were made in the servants' quarters and at the stables, but they were not there. A search was made in the village, but they could not be found. At teatime they were still missing, and when the family had to sit down to supper without them, Mama was terribly anxious and was even crying. That night another search was made in the village and men were sent down to the river with lanterns. Heavens, what an uproar arose!

Next morning the policeman arrived and went into the dining room to write something. Mama was crying.

Suddenly, lo and behold!, a posting sleigh drove up to the front door with clouds of steam rising from its three white horses.

"Volodia is here!" cried someone in the courtyard.

"Volodichka is here!" shrieked Natalia, rushing into the dining room.

Milord barked in his deep voice.

It seemed that the boys had been stopped at the hotel in the town, where they had gone about asking every one where they could buy gunpowder. As he entered the hall, Volodia burst into tears and flung his arms round his mother's neck. The girls trembled with terror at the thought of what would happen next, for they heard Papa call Volodia and Chechevitsyn into his study and begin talking to them. Mama wept and joined in the talk.

"Do you think it was right?" Papa asked, chiding them. "I hope to goodness they won't find out at school, because, if they do, you will certainly be expelled. Be ashamed of yourself, Master Chechevitsin! You are a bad boy. You are a mischief-maker and your parents will punish you. Do you think it was right to run away? Where did you spend the night?"

"In the station!" answered Chechevitsyn proudly.

Volodia was put to bed, and a towel soaked in vinegar was laid on his head. A telegram was dispatched, and the next day a lady arrived, Chechevitsin's mother, who took her son away.

As Chechevitsyn departed his face looked haughty and stern. He said not a word as he took his leave of the girls, but in a school notebook of Katia's he wrote these words for remembrance:

"Montehomo, the Hawk's Claw."

1887

A CHRISTMAS TREE AND A WEDDING

Fyodor Dostoevsky

The other day I saw a wedding ... but no, I had better tell you about the Christmas tree. The wedding was nice, I liked it very much, but the other incident was better. I don't know how it was that, looking at that wedding, I thought of that Christmas tree. This was what happened. Just five years ago, on New Year's Eve, I was invited to a children's party. The giver of the party was a well-known and businesslike personage, with connections, a large circle of acquaintances, and a good many schemes on hand, so it may be supposed that this party was an excuse for getting the parents together and discussing various interesting matters in an innocent, casual way. I was an outsider; I had no interesting matter to contribute, and so I spent the evening rather independently. There was another gentleman present who was, I fancied, of no special rank or family, and who, like me, had simply turned up at this family festivity. He was the first to catch my eye. He was a tall, lanky man, very grave and very correctly dressed. But one could see that he was in no mood for merrymaking and family festivity. Whenever he withdrew into a corner he left off smiling and knitted his bushy black brows. He had not a single acquaintance in the party except his host. One could see that he was fearfully bored, but that he was valiantly keeping up the part of a man perfectly happy and enjoying himself. I learned afterward that this was a gentleman from the provinces with a critical and perplexing piece of business in Petersburg, who had brought a letter of introduction to our host, and whom our host was, by no means con amore, patronizing, and whom he had invited, out of civility, to his children's party. He did not play cards, cigars were not offered him, everyone avoided entering into conversation with him, most likely recognizing the bird from its feathers; and so my gentleman was forced to sit the whole evening stroking his whiskers simply to have something to do with his hands. His whiskers were certainly very fine. But he stroked them so zealously that, looking at him, one might have supposed that the whiskers were created first and the gentleman was only attached later in order to stroke them.

In addition to this individual who assisted in this way at our host's family festivity (he had five fat, well-fed boys), I was attracted, too, by another gentleman. But he was quite of a different sort. He was a personage. He was called Yulian Mastakovitch. From the first glance one could see that he was an honored guest, and stood in the same relation to our host as our host stood in relation to the gentleman who was stroking his whiskers. Our host and hostess said no end of polite things to him, waited on him hand and foot, pressed him to drink, flattered him, brought their visitors up to be introduced to him, but did not take him to be introduced to anyone else. I noticed tears glistened in our host's eyes when he remarked about the party that he had rarely spent an evening so agreeably. I felt, as it were, frightened in the presence of such a personage, and so, after admiring the children, I went away into a little parlor, which was quite empty, and sat down in an arbor of flowers which filled up almost half the room.

The children were all incredibly sweet, and resolutely refused to model themselves on the grown-ups, regardless of all the admonitions of their governesses and mamas. They stripped the Christmas tree to the last candy in the twinkling of an eye, and had succeeded in breaking half the playthings before they knew what was destined for whom. Particularly charming was a black-eyed, curly-headed boy, who kept trying to shoot me with his wooden gun. But my attention was still more attracted by his sister, a girl of eleven, quiet, pensive, pale, with big, prominent, pensive eyes, exquisite as a little Cupid. The children hurt her feelings in some way, and so she came away from them to the same empty parlor in which I was sitting, and played with her doll in the corner. The visitors respectfully pointed out her father, a wealthy contractor, and someone whispered that three hundred thousand rubles were already set aside for her dowry. I turned around to glance at the group who were interested in such a circumstance, and my eye fell on Yulian Mastakovitch, who, with his hands behind his back and his head on one side, was listening with the greatest attention to the gentlemen's idle gossip. Afterward I could not help admiring the discrimination of the host and hostess in the distribution of the children's presents. The little girl, who had already a portion of three hundred thousand rubles, received the costliest doll. Then followed presents diminishing in value in accordance with the rank of the parents of these happy children; finally, the child of lowest degree, a thin, freckled, red-haired little boy of ten, got nothing but a book of stories about the marvels of nature and tears of devotion, etc., without pictures or even woodcuts. He was the son of a poor widow, the governess of the children of the house, an oppressed and scared little boy. He was dressed in a short jacket of inferior nankeen. After receiving his book he walked around the other toys for a long time; he longed to play with the other children, but did not dare; it was evident that he already felt and understood his position. I love watching children. Their first independent approaches to life are extremely interesting. I noticed that the red-haired boy was so fascinated by the costly toys of the other children, especially by a theater in which he certainly longed to take some part, that he made up his mind to sacrifice his dignity. He smiled and began playing with the other children, he gave away his apple to a fat-faced little boy who had a mass of goodies tied up in a pocket handkerchief already, and even brought himself to carry another boy on his back, simply not to be turned away from the theater, but an insolent youth gave him a heavy thump a minute later. The child did not dare to cry. Then the governess, his mother, made her appearance, and told him not to interfere with the other children's playing. The boy went away to the same room where the little girl was. She let him join her, and the two set to work very eagerly dressing the expensive doll.

I had been sitting more than half an hour in the ivy arbor, listening to the little prattle of the red-haired boy and the beauty with the dowry of three hundred thousand, who was nursing her doll, when Yulian Mastakovitch suddenly walked into the room. He had taken advantage of the general commotion following a quarrel among the children to step out of the drawing room. I had noticed him a moment before talking very cordially to the future heiress's papa, whose acquaintance he had just made, about the superiority of one branch of the service over another. Now he stood in hesitation and seemed to be reckoning something on his fingers.

"Three hundred ... three hundred," he was whispering. "Eleven ... twelve ... thirteen," and so on. "Sixteen—five years! Supposing it is at four per cent—five times twelve is sixty; yes, to that sixty ... well, in five years we may assume it will be four hundred. Yes! ... But he won't stick to four per cent, the rascal. He can get eight or ten. Well, five hundred, let us say, five hundred at least ... that's certain; well, say a little more for frills. Hmm! ..."

His hesitation was at an end, he blew his nose and was on the point of going out of the room when he suddenly glanced at the little girl and stopped short. He did not see me behind the pots of greenery. It seemed to me that he was greatly excited. Either his calculations had affected his imagination or something else, for he rubbed his hands and could hardly stand still. This excitement reached its utmost limit when he stopped and bent another resolute glance at the future heiress. He was about to move forward, but first looked around, then moving on tiptoe, as though he felt guilty, he advanced towards the children. He approached with a little smile, bent down, and kissed her on the head. The child, not expecting this attack, uttered a cry of alarm.

"What are you doing here, sweet child?" he asked in a whisper, looking around and patting the girl's cheek.

"We are playing."

"Ah! With him?" Yulian Mastakovitch looked askance at the boy. "You had better go into the drawing room, my dear," he said to him.

The boy looked at him open-eyed and did not utter a word. Yulian Mastakovitch looked around again, and again bent down to the little girl.

"And what is this you've got—a dolly, dear child?" he asked.

"Yes, a dolly," answered the girl, frowning, and a little shy.

"A dolly ... And do you know, dear child, what your dolly is made of?"

"I don't know ..." the little girl answered in a whisper, hanging her head.

"It's made of rags, darling. You had better go into the drawing room to your playmates, boy," said Yulian Mastakovitch, looking sternly at the boy.

The boy and girl frowned and clutched at each other. They did not want to be separated.

"And do you know why they gave you that doll?" asked Yulian Mastakovitch, dropping his voice to a softer and softer tone.

"I don't know."

"Because you have been a sweet and well-behaved child all the week."

At this point Yulian Mastakovitch, more excited than ever, speaking in most dulcet tones, asked at last, in a hardly audible voice choked with emotion and impatience:

"And will you love me, dear little girl, when I come and see your papa and mama?"

Saying this, Yulian Mastakovitch tried once more to kiss "the dear little girl," but the red-haired boy, seeing that the little girl was on the point of tears, clutched her hand and began whimpering from sympathy for her. Yulian Mastakovitch was angry in earnest.

"Go away, go away from here, go away!" he said to the boy. "Go into the drawing room! Go in there to your playmates!"

"No, he doesn't have to, he doesn't have to! You go away," said the little girl. "Leave him alone, leave him alone," she said, almost crying.

Someone made a sound at the door. Yulian Mastakovitch instantly raised his majestic person and took alarm. But the red-haired boy was even more alarmed than Yulian Mastakovitch; he abandoned the little girl and, slinking along by the wall, stole out of the parlor into the dining room. To avoid arousing suspicion, Yulian Mastakovitch, too, went into the dining room. He was as red as a lobster, and, glancing into the looking glass, seemed to be ashamed at himself. He was perhaps vexed with himself for his impetuosity and hastiness. Possibly, he was at first so much impressed by his calculations, so inspired and fascinated by them, that in spite of his seriousness and dignity he made up his mind to behave like a boy, and directly approach the object of his attentions, even though she could not be really the object of his attentions for another five years at least. I followed the estimable gentleman into the dining room and there beheld a strange spectacle. Yulian Mastakovitch, flushed with vexation and anger, was frightening the red-haired boy, who, retreating from him, did not know where to run in his terror.

"Go away! What are you doing here? Go away, you scamp. Are you after the fruit here, eh? Get along, you naughty boy! Get along, you sniveler, to your playmates!"

The panic-stricken boy in his desperation tried creeping under the table. Then his persecutor, in a fury, took out his large batiste handkerchief and began flicking it under the table at the child, who kept perfectly quiet. It must be observed that Yulian Mastakovitch was a little inclined to be fat. He was a sleek, red-faced, solidly built man, paunchy, with thick legs; what is called a fine figure of a man, round as a nut. He was perspiring, breathless, and fearfully flushed. At last he was almost rigid, so great was his indignation and perhaps—who knows?—his jealousy. I burst into loud laughter. Yulian Mastakovitch turned around and, in spite of all his consequence, was overcome with confusion. At that moment from the opposite door our host came in. The boy crept out from under the table and wiped his elbows and his knees. Yulian Mastakovitch hastened to put to his nose the handkerchief which he was holding in his hand by one end.

Our host looked at the three of us in some perplexity, but as a man who knew something of life, and looked at it from a serious point of view, he at once availed himself of the chance of catching his visitor by himself.

"Here, this is the boy," he said, pointing to the red-haired boy, "for whom I had the honor to solicit your influence."

"Ah!" said Yulian Mastakovitch, who had hardly quite recovered himself.

"The son of my children's governess," said our host, in a tone of a petitioner, "a poor woman, the widow of an honest civil servant; and therefore ... and therefore, Yulian Mastakovitch, if it were possible ..."

"Oh, no, no!" Yulian Mastakovitch made haste to answer. "No, excuse me, Filipp Alexeevitch, it's quite impossible. I've made inquiries; there's no vacancy, and if there were, there are twenty applicants who have far more claim than he ... I am very sorry, very sorry ..."

"What a pity," said our host. "He is a quiet, well-behaved boy."

"A great rascal, as I notice," answered Yulian Mastakovitch, with a nervous twist of his lip. "Get along, boy, why are you standing there? Go to your playmates," he said, addressing the child.

At that point he could not contain himself, and glanced at me out of one eye. I, too, could not contain myself, and laughed straight in his face. Yulian Mastakovitch turned away at once, and in a voice calculated to reach my ear, asked who was that strange young man? They whispered together and walked out of the room. I saw Yulian Mastakovitch afterward shaking his head incredulously as our host talked to him.

After laughing to my heart's content I returned to the drawing room. There the great man, surrounded by fathers and mothers of families, including the host and hostess, was saying something very warmly to a lady to whom he had just been introduced. The lady was holding by the hand the little girl with whom Yulian Mastakovitch had had the scene in the parlor a little while before. Now he was launching into praises and raptures over the beauty, the talents, the grace, and the charming manners of the darling little child. He was unmistakably ingratiating himself to the mama. The mother listened to him almost with tears of delight. The father's lips were smiling. Our host was delighted at the general satisfaction. All the guests, in fact, were sympathetically gratified; even the children's games were checked that they might not hinder the conversation: the whole atmosphere was saturated with reverence. I heard afterward the mother of the interesting child, deeply touched, beg Yulian Mastakovitch, in carefully chosen phrases, to do her the special honor of bestowing upon them the precious gift of his acquaintance, and heard with what unaffected delight Yulian Mastakovitch accepted the invitation, and how afterward the guests, dispersing in different directions, moving away with the greatest propriety, poured out to one another the most touchingly flattering comments upon the contractor, his wife, his little girl, and, above all, upon Yulian Mastakovitch.

"Is that gentleman married?" I asked, almost aloud, of one of my acquaintances, who was standing nearest to Yulian Mastakovitch. Yulian Mastakovitch flung a searching and vindictive glance at me.

"No!" answered my acquaintance, chagrined to the bottom of his heart by the awkwardness of which I had intentionally been guilty ...

I passed lately by a certain church; I was struck by the crowd of people in carriages. I heard people talking of a wedding. It was a cloudy day, it was beginning to sleet. I made my way through the crowd at the door and saw the bridegroom. He was a sleek, well-fed, round, paunchy man, very gorgeously dressed up. He was running fussily about, giving orders. At last the news passed through the crowd that the bride was coming. I squeezed my way through the crowd and saw a marvelous beauty who could scarcely have reached her first season. But the beauty was pale and melancholy. She looked preoccupied; I even fancied that her eyes were red with recent weeping. The classic severity of every feature of her face gave a certain dignity and seriousness to her beauty. But through that sternness and dignity, through that melancholy, could be seen the look of childish innocence, something indescribably naïve, fluid, youthful, which seemed mutely begging for mercy.

People were saying that she was only just sixteen. Glancing attentively at the bridegroom, I suddenly recognized him as Yulian Mastakovitch, whom I had not seen for five years. I looked at her. My God! I began to squeeze my way as quickly as I could out of the church. I heard people saying in the crowd that the bride was an heiress, that she had a dowry of five hundred thousand ... and a trousseau worth ever so much.

"The calculation was correct, though!" I thought as I made my way into the street.

1848

AT CHRISTMASTIDE

Anton Chekhov

"What shall I write?" said Yegor, and he dipped his pen in the ink.

Vasilisa had not seen her daughter for four years. Her daughter, Yefimya, had gone after her wedding to Petersburg, had sent them two letters, and since then seemed to vanish out of their lives—there had been no sight or sound of her. And whether the old woman was milking her cow at dawn, or heating her stove, or dozing at night, she was always thinking of one and the same thing—what was happening to Yefimya, whether she was alive out yonder. She ought to have sent a letter, but the old father could not write, and there was no one to write.

But now Christmas had come, and Vasilisa could not bear it any longer, and went to the tavern to Yegor, the brother of the innkeeper's wife, who had sat in the tavern doing nothing ever since he came back from the army. People said that he could write letters very well if he were properly paid. Vasilisa talked to the cook at the tavern, then to the mistress of the house, then to Yegor himself. They agreed upon fifteen kopecks.

And now—it happened on the second day of the holidays, in the tavern kitchen—Yegor was sitting at the table, holding the pen in his hand. Vasilisa was standing before him, pondering with an expression of anxiety and woe on her face. Pyotr, her husband, a very thin old man with a brownish bald patch, had come with her. He stood looking straight before him like a blind man. On the stove a piece of pork was being braised in a saucepan; it was spurting and hissing, and seemed to be actually saying: "Flu-flu-flu." It was stifling.

"What am I to write?" Yegor asked again.

"What?" asked Vasilisa, looking at him angrily and suspiciously. "Don't worry me! You are not writing for nothing. No fear, you'll be paid for it. Come, write: 'To our dear son-in-law, Andrei Khrisanfitch, and to our only beloved daughter, Yefimya Petrovna, with our love we send a low bow and our parental blessing abiding for ever.'"

"Written. Fire away."

"And we wish them a happy Christmas, we are alive and well, and I wish you the same, please the Lord … the Heavenly King."

Vasilisa pondered and exchanged glances with the old man.

"And I wish you the same, please the Lord the Heavenly King," she repeated, beginning to cry.

She could say nothing more. And yet before, when she lay awake thinking at night, it had seemed to her that she could not get all she had to say into a dozen letters. Since the time when her daughter had gone away with her husband much water had flowed into the sea, the old people had lived feeling bereaved, and sighed heavily at night as though they had buried their daughter. And how many events had occurred in the village since then, how many marriages and deaths! How long the winters had been! How long the nights!

"It's hot," said Yegor, unbuttoning his waistcoat. "It must be a hundred degrees. What more?" he asked.

The old people were silent.

"What does your son-in-law do in Petersburg?" asked Yegor.

"He was a soldier, uncle," the old man answered in a weak voice. "He left the service at the same time as you did. He was a soldier, and now, to be sure, he is at Petersburg at a hydropathic establishment. The doctor treats the sick with water. So he, to be sure, is house porter at the doctor's."

"Here it is written down," said the old woman, taking a letter out of her pocket. "We got it from Yefimya, goodness knows when. Maybe they are no longer in this world."

Yegor thought a little and began writing rapidly:

"At the present time," he wrote, "since your destiny through your own doing allotted you to the Military Career, we counsel you to look into the Code of Disciplinary Offenses and Fundamental Laws of the War Office, and you will see in that law the Civilization of the Officials of the War Office."

He wrote and kept reading aloud what was written, while Vasilisa considered what she ought to say: how great had been their want the year before, how their corn had not lasted even till Christmas, how they had to sell their cow. She ought to ask for money, ought to write that the old father was often ailing and would soon no doubt give up his soul to God … but how to express this in words? What must be said first and what afterward?

"Take note," Yegor went on writing, "in volume five of the Army Regulations soldier is a common noun and a proper one, a soldier of the first rank is called a general, and of the last a private …"

The old man stirred his lips and said softly:

"It would be all right to have a look at the grandchildren."

"What grandchildren?" asked the old woman, and she looked angrily at him. "Perhaps there are none."

"Well, but perhaps there are. Who knows?"

"And thereby you can judge," Yegor hurried on, "what is the enemy without and what is the enemy within. The foremost of our enemies within is Bacchus." The pen squeaked, executing upon the paper flourishes like fish-hooks. Yegor hastened and read over every line several times. He sat on a stool sprawling his broad feet under the table, well-fed, bursting with health, with a coarse animal face and a red bull neck. He was vulgarity itself: coarse, conceited, invincible, proud of having been born and bred in a pothouse, and Vasilisa quite understood the vulgarity, but could not express it in words, and could look only angrily and suspiciously at Yegor. Her head was beginning to ache, and her thoughts were in confusion from the sound of his voice and his unintelligible words, from the heat and the stuffiness, and she said nothing and thought nothing, but simply waited for him to finish scribbling. But the old man looked with full confidence. He believed in his old woman who had brought him there, and in Yegor, and when he had mentioned the hydropathic establishment it could be seen that he believed in the establishment and the healing efficacy of water.

Having finished the letter, Yegor got up and read the whole of it through from the beginning. The old man did not understand, but he nodded his head trustfully.

"That's all right; it is smooth …" he said. "God give you health. That's all right …"

They laid on the table three five-kopeck pieces and went out of the tavern. The old man looked immovably straight before him as though he were blind, and perfect trustfulness was written on his face, but as Vasilisa came out of the tavern she raised her arms threateningly at the dog, and said angrily:

"Akh, the plague."

The old woman did not sleep all night, she was disturbed by thoughts, and at daybreak she got up, said her prayers, and went to the station to send off the letter.

It was between eight and nine miles to the station.

II

Dr. B. O. Mozelweiser's hydropathic establishment worked on New Year's Day exactly as on ordinary days. The only difference was that the porter, Andrei Khrisanfitch, had on a uniform with new braiding, his boots had an extra polish, and he greeted every visitor with "A Happy New Year to you!"

It was the morning. Andrei Khrisanfitch was standing at the door, reading the newspaper. Just at ten o'clock there arrived a general, one of the habitual visitors, and directly after him the postman. Andrei Khrisanfitch helped the general off with his greatcoat, and said:

"A Happy New Year to Your Excellency!"

"Thank you, my good fellow. The same to you."

And at the top of the stairs the general asked, nodding toward the door (he asked the same question every day and always forgot the answer):

"And what is there in that room?"

"The massage room, Your Excellency."

When the general's steps had died away Andrei Khrisanfitch looked at the post that had come, and found one addressed to himself. He tore it open, read several lines, then, looking at the newspaper, he walked without haste to his own room, which was downstairs close by at the end of the passage. His wife, Yefimya, was sitting on the bed, feeding her baby; another child, the eldest, was standing by, laying its curly head on her knee; a third was asleep on the bed.

Going into the room, Andrei gave his wife the letter and said:

"From the country, I suppose."

Then he walked out again without taking his eyes from the paper. He could hear Yefimya with a shaking voice reading the first lines. She read them and could read no more; these lines were enough for her. She burst into tears, and hugging her eldest child, kissing him, she began saying—and it was hard to say whether she were laughing or crying:

"It's from granny, from grandfather," she said. "From the country ... The Heavenly Mother, Saints, and Martyrs! The snow lies heaped up under the roofs now ... the trees are as white as white. The boys slide on little sledges ... and dear old bald grandfather is on the stove ... and there is a little yellow dog ... My own darlings!"

Andrei Khrisanfitch, hearing this, recalled that his wife had on three or four occasions given him letters and asked him to send them to the country, but some important business had always prevented him; he had not sent them, and the letters somehow got lost.

"And little hares run about in the fields," Yefimya went on chanting, kissing her boy and shedding tears. "Grandfather is kind and gentle, granny is good, too, and kind-hearted. They are warmhearted in the country, they are God-fearing ... and there is a little church in the village, the peasants sing in the choir. Queen of Heaven, Holy Mother and Defender, take us away from here!"

Andrei Khrisanfitch returned to his room to smoke a little till there was another ring at the door, and Yefimya ceased speaking, subsided, and wiped her eyes, though her lips were still quivering. She was very much frightened of him—oh, how frightened of him! She trembled and was reduced to terror by the sound of his steps, by the look in his eyes, and dared not utter a word in his presence.

Andrei Khrisanfitch lighted a cigarette, but at that very moment there was a ring from upstairs. He put out his cigarette, and, assuming a very grave face, hastened to his front door.

The general was coming downstairs, fresh and rosy from his bath.

"And what is there in that room?" he asked, pointing to a door.

Andrei Khrisanfitch put his hands down swiftly to the seams of his trousers, and pronounced loudly:

"A Charcot douche, Your Excellency!

1900

DREAM OF THE YOUNG TSAR

Lev Tolstoy

The young Tsar had just ascended the throne. For five weeks he had worked without ceasing, in the way that Tsars are accustomed to work. He had been attending to reports, signing papers, receiving ambassadors and high officials who came to be presented to him, and reviewing troops. He was tired, and as a traveller exhausted by heat and thirst longs for water and for rest, so he longed for a respite of just one day at least from receptions, from speeches, from parades—a few free hours to spend like an ordinary human being with his young, clever, and beautiful wife, to whom he had been married only a month before.

It was Christmas Eve. The young Tsar had arranged to have a complete rest that evening. The night before he had worked till very late at documents that his ministers of state had left for him to examine. In the morning he was present at matins and then at a military service. In the afternoon he received official visitors; and later he had been obliged to listen to the reports of ministers of state, and had given his assent to many important matters. In his conference with the Minister of Finance he had agreed to an increase of duties on imported goods, which should in the future add many millions to the State revenues. Then he sanctioned the sale of brandy by the Crown in various parts of the country, and signed a decree permitting the sale of alcohol in villages having markets. This was also calculated to increase the principal revenue to the State, which was derived from the sale of spirits. He had also approved of the issuing of a new gold loan required for a financial negotiation. The Minister of Justice having reported on the complicated case of the succession of the Baron Snyders, the young Tsar confirmed the decision by his signature, and also approved the new rules relating to the application of Article 1830 of the penal code, providing for the punishment of tramps. In his conference with the Minister of the Interior he ratified the order concerning the collection of taxes in arrears, signed the order settling what measures should be taken in regard to the persecution of religious dissenters, and also one providing for the continuance of martial law in those provinces where it had already been established. With the Minister of War he arranged for the nomination of a new Corps Commander for the raising of recruits, and for punishment of breach of discipline. These things kept him occupied till dinnertime, and even then his freedom was not complete. A number of high officials had been invited to dinner, and he was obliged to talk to them—not in the way he felt disposed to do, but according to what he was expected to say. At last the tiresome dinner was over, and the guests departed.

The young Tsar heaved a sigh of relief, stretched himself, and retired to his apartments to take off his uniform with the decorations on it, and to don the jacket he used to wear before his accession to the throne. His young wife had also retired to take off her dinner dress, remarking that she would join him presently.

When he had passed the row of footmen who were standing erect before him, and reached his room, when he had thrown off his heavy uniform and put on his jacket, the young Tsar felt glad to be free from work, and his heart was filled with a tender emotion which sprang from the consciousness of his freedom, of his joyous, robust young life, and of his love. He threw himself on the sofa, stretched out his legs upon it, leaned his head on his hand, fixed his gaze on the dull glass shade of the lamp, and then a sensation that he had not experienced since his childhood—the pleasure of going to sleep, and a drowsiness that was irresistible—suddenly came over him.

"My wife will be here presently and will find me asleep. No, I must not go to sleep," he thought. He let his elbow drop down, laid his cheek in the palm of his hand, made himself comfortable, and was so utterly happy that he felt only a desire not to be aroused from this delightful state.

And then what happens to all of us every day happened to him—he fell asleep without knowing himself when or how. He passed from one state into another without his will having any share in it, without even desiring it, and without regretting the state out of which he had passed. He fell into a heavy sleep which was like death. How long he had slept he did not know, but he was suddenly aroused by the soft touch of a hand upon his shoulder.

"It is my darling, it is she," he thought. "What a shame to have dozed off!"

But it was not she. Before his eyes, which were wide open and blinking at the light, she, that charming and beautiful creature whom he was expecting, did not stand, but he stood. Who he was the young Tsar did not know, but somehow it did not strike him that he was a stranger whom he had never seen before. It seemed as if he had known him for a long time and was fond of him, and as if he trusted him as he would trust himself. He had expected his beloved wife, but in her stead that man whom he had never seen before had come. Yet to the young Tsar, who was far from feeling regret or astonishment, it seemed not only a most natural, but also a necessary thing to happen.

"Come!" said the stranger.

"Yes, let us go," said the young Tsar, not knowing where he was to go, but quite aware that he could not help submitting to the command of the stranger. "But how shall we go?" he asked.

"This is how."

The stranger laid his hand on the Tsar's head, and the Tsar for a moment lost consciousness.

He could not tell whether he had been unconscious a long or a short time, but when he recovered his senses he found himself in an open field on the wide frontier.

On the right were potato fields; the plants had been rooted out, and were lying in heaps, blackened by the frost; in alternate streaks were rows of winter corn. In the distance a little village with its tiled roofs was visible; on the left were fields of winter corn, and fields of stubble. No one was to be seen on any side, save a black human figure in front at the borderline, a gun slung on his back, and at his feet a dog. On the spot where the young Tsar stood, sitting beside him, almost at his feet, was a young Russian soldier with a green band on his cap and with his rifle slung over his shoulders, who was rolling up a paper to make a cigarette. The soldier was obviously unaware of the presence of the young Tsar and his companion, and had not heard them. He did not turn around when the Tsar, who was standing directly over the soldier, asked, "Where are we?"

"On the Prussian frontier," his companion answered.

Suddenly, far away in front of them, a shot was fired. The soldier jumped to his feet, and seeing two men running, bent low to the ground, hastily put his tobacco into his pocket, and ran after one of them. "Stop, or I'll shoot!" cried the soldier. The fugitive, without stopping, turned his head and called out something evidently abusive or blasphemous.

"Damn you!" shouted the soldier, who put one foot a little forward and stopped, after which, bending his head over his rifle, and raising his right hand, he rapidly adjusted something, took aim, and, pointing the gun in the direction of the fugitive, probably fired, although no sound was heard. "Smokeless powder, no doubt," thought the young Tsar, and looking after the fleeing man saw him take a few hurried steps, and bending lower and lower, fall to the ground and crawl on his hands and knees. At last he remained lying and did not move. The other fugitive, who was ahead of him, turned around and ran back to the man who was lying on the ground. He did something for him and then resumed his flight.

"What does all this mean?" asked the Tsar.

"These are the guards on the frontier, enforcing the revenue laws. That man was killed to protect the revenues of the State."

"Has he actually been killed?"

The companion again laid his hand upon the head of the young Tsar, and again the Tsar lost consciousness. When he had recovered his senses he found himself in a small room—the customs office. The dead body of a man, with a thin grizzled beard, an aquiline nose, and big eyes with the eyelids closed, was lying on the floor. His arms were thrown asunder, his feet bare, and his thick, dirty toes were turned up at right angles and stuck straight up. He had a wound in his side, and on his ragged cloth jacket, as well as on his blue shirt, were stains of clotted blood, which had turned black save for a few red spots here and there. A woman stood close to the wall, so wrapped up in shawls that her face could scarcely be seen. Motionless she gazed at the aquiline nose, the upturned feet, and the protruding eyeballs, sobbing and sighing, and drying her tears at long, regular intervals. A pretty girl of thirteen was standing at her mother's side, with her eyes and mouth wide open. A boy of six clung to his mother's skirt, and looked intensely at his dead father without blinking.

From a door near them an official, an officer, a doctor, and a clerk with documents, entered. After them came a soldier, the one who had shot the man. He stepped briskly along behind his superiors, but the instant he saw the corpse he went suddenly pale, and quivered, and dropping his head, he stood still. When the official asked him whether that was the man who was escaping across the frontier, and at whom he had fired, he was unable to answer. His lips trembled, and his face twitched. "Yes—s—s—s—" he began, but could not get out the words that he wanted to say. "Yes sir, Your Excellency." The officials looked at one another and wrote something down.

"And here you'll see the beneficial results of that same system," the companion said:

In a room of sumptuous vulgarity two men sat drinking wine. One of them was old and gray, the other a young Jew. The young Jew was holding a roll of banknotes in his hand, and was bargaining with the old man. He was buying smuggled goods.

"You've got 'em cheap," he said, smiling.

"Yes—but the risk—"

"This is indeed terrible," said the young Tsar, "but it can hardly be avoided. Such proceedings are necessary."

His companion made no response, saying merely, "Let us move on," and laid his hand again on the head of the Tsar. When the Tsar recovered consciousness, he was standing in a small room lit by a shaded lamp. A woman was sitting at the table sewing. A boy of eight was bending over the table, drawing, with his feet doubled up under him in the armchair. A student was reading aloud. The father and daughter of the family entered the room noisily.

"You signed the order concerning the sale of spirits," said the companion to the Tsar.

"Well?" said the woman.

"He's not likely to live."

"What's the matter with him?"

"They've poisoned him with wine."

"It's not possible!" exclaimed the wife.

"It's true. And the boy's only nine years old, that Vania Moroshkin."

"What did you do to try to save him?" asked the wife.

"I tried everything that could be done. I gave him an emetic and put a mustard plaster on him. He has every symptom of delirium tremens."

"It's no wonder—the whole family are drunkards. Anisia is only a little better than the rest, and even she is generally more or less drunk," said the daughter.

"And what about your temperance society?" the student asked his sister.

"What can we do when they are given every opportunity of drinking? Father tried to have the public house shut down, but the law is against him. And, besides, when I was trying to convince Vasily Ermilin that it was disgraceful to keep a public house and ruin the people with drink, he answered very haughtily, and indeed got the better of me before the crowd: 'But I have a license with the Imperial eagle on it. If there was anything wrong in my business, the Tsar wouldn't have issued a decree authorizing it.' Isn't it terrible? The whole village has been drunk for the last three days. And as for feast days, it is simply horrible to think of! It has been proved conclusively that alcohol does no good in any case, but invariably does harm, and it has been demonstrated to be an absolute poison. Then, ninety-nine percent of the crimes in the world are committed through its influence. We all know how the standard of morality and the general welfare improved at once in all the countries where drinking has been suppressed—like Sweden and Finland, and we know that it can be suppressed by exercising a moral influence over the masses. But in our country the class which could exert that influence—the Government, the Tsar and his officials—simply encourage drink. Their main revenues are drawn from the continual drunkenness of the people. They drink themselves—they are always drinking the health of somebody: 'Gentlemen, the Regiment!' The priests drink, the bishops drink—"

Again the guide touched the head of the young Tsar, who again lost consciousness. This time he found himself in a peasant's cottage. The peasant—a man of forty, with red face and bloodshot eyes—was furiously striking the face of an old man, who tried in vain to protect himself from the blows. The younger peasant seized the beard of the old man and held it fast.

"For shame! To strike your father—!"

"I don't care, I'll kill him! Let them send me to Siberia, I don't care!"

The women were screaming. Drunken officials rushed into the cottage and separated father and son. The father had an arm broken and the son's beard was torn out. In the doorway a drunken girl was offering herself up to an old drunken peasant.

"They are beasts!" said the young Tsar.

"No, they are children."

Another touch of the hand and the young Tsar awoke in a new place. It was the office of the justice of the peace. A fat, bald-headed man, with a double chin and a chain around his neck, had just risen from his seat, and was reading the sentence in a loud voice, while a crowd of peasants stood behind the grating. There was a woman in rags in the crowd who did not rise. The guard gave her a push.

"Asleep! I tell you to stand up!" The woman rose.

"According to the decree of his Imperial Majesty—" the judge began reading the sentence. The case concerned that very woman. She had taken away half a bundle of oats as she was passing the threshing-floor of a landowner. The justice of the peace sentenced her to two months' imprisonment. The landowner whose oats had been stolen was among the audience. When the judge adjourned the court the landowner approached, and shook hands, and the judge entered into conversation with him. The next case was about a stolen samovar. Then there was a trial about some timber which had been cut, to the detriment of the landowner. Some peasants were being tried for having assaulted the constable of the district.

When the young Tsar again lost consciousness, he awoke to find himself in the middle of a village, where he saw hungry, half-frozen children and the wife of one of the men who had assaulted the constable, broken down from overwork.

Then came a new scene. In Siberia, a tramp is being flogged with the lash, the direct result of an order issued by the Minister of Justice. Again oblivion, and another scene. The family of a Jewish watchmaker is evicted for being too poor. The little Jew children are crying, and the Jew, Isaak, is greatly distressed. At last they come to an arrangement, and he is allowed to stay on in the lodgings.

The chief of police takes a bribe. The governor of the province also secretly accepts a bribe. Taxes are being collected. In the village, while a cow is sold for payment, the police inspector is bribed by a factory owner, who thus escapes taxes altogether. And again a village court scene, and a sentence carried into execution—the lash!

"Ilya Vasilievich, could you not spare me that?"

"No."

The peasant burst into tears. "Christ suffered, and He's willed it thus."

Then other scenes. The Shtundists—Evangelical Christians outlawed by the government—being broken up and dispersed; the clergy refusing first to marry, then to bury a Protestant. Orders given concerning the passage of the Imperial railway train. Soldiers kept sitting in the mud—cold, hungry, and cursing. Decrees issued relating to the educational institutions under the tutelage of Tsarina Maria. Corruption rampant in the orphanages. An undeserved monument. Thieving among the clergy. The reinforcement of the political police. A woman being searched. A prison for convicts who are sentenced to be deported. A man being hanged for murdering a shop assistant.

Then the result of military discipline: soldiers wearing uniform and scoffing at it. A gypsy encampment. The son of a millionaire exempted from military duty, while the only support of a large family is forced to serve. The university: a teacher relieved of military service, while the most gifted musicians are compelled. Soldiers and their debauchery—and the spreading of syphilis.

Then a soldier who has made an attempt to desert. He is being tried. Another is on trial for striking an officer who has insulted his mother. He is put to death. Others, again, are tried for having refused to shoot. The runaway soldier sent to a disciplinary battalion and flogged to death. Another, who is guiltless, flogged, and his wounds sprinkled with salt till he dies. And soldiers' pay: nothing but drink, debauchery, cards, and arrogance.

Meanwhile, this is the general condition of the people: the children are starving and of degenerate families, the houses are full of animals, mind-numbing labor, submission, and sadness. On the other hand: ministers, governors—

greedy, ambitious, and filled with vanity and concern for acquiring importance and instilling fear.

"But where are the people?"

"I will show you where they are: men in exile, alone, frozen or eaten with resentment. In hard labor, where women are flogged. A woman prisoner in Shlusselburg in solitary confinement, going mad. And here's another woman, a girl, in her time, violated by soldiers."

"Are there many?"

"Tens of thousands of the best people. Some shut up in prisons, others ruined by false education, by the vain desire to bring them up as we wish. But not succeeding in this, whatever might have been is ruined as well, for it is made impossible. It is as if we were trying to make buckwheat out of corn sprouts by splitting the ears. One may spoil the corn, but one could never change it to buckwheat. Thus all the youth of the world, the entire younger generation, is being ruined. But woe to those who destroy one of these little ones, woe to you if you destroy even one of them. On your soul, however, are hosts of them, who have been ruined in your name, all of those over whom your power extends."

"But what can I do?" exclaimed the Tsar in despair. "I do not wish to torture, to flog, to corrupt, to kill anyone! I only want the welfare of all. Just as I yearn for happiness myself, so I want the world to be happy as well. Am I actually responsible for everything that is done in my name? What can I do? What am I to do to rid myself of such a responsibility? What can I do? I do not admit that the responsibility for all this is mine. If I felt myself responsible for one-hundredth part of it, I would shoot myself on the spot. It would not be possible to live if that were true. But how can I put an end to all this evil? It is bound up with the very existence of the State. I am the head of the State! What am I to do? Kill myself? Or abdicate? But that would mean renouncing my duty. O God, O God, God, help me!" He burst into tears and awoke.

"How glad I am that it was only a dream," was his first thought. But when he began to recollect what he had seen in his dream, and to compare it with actuality, he realized that the problem propounded to him in dream remained just as important and as insoluble now that he was awake. For the first time the young Tsar became aware of the heavy responsibility weighing on him, and was aghast. His thoughts no longer turned to the young Tsarina and to the happiness he had anticipated for that evening, but became centered on the unanswerable question that hung over him: "What was to be done?"

In a state of great agitation he arose and went into the next room. An old courtier, an official and friend of his deceased father's, was standing there in the middle of the room in conversation with the young Tsarina, who was on her way to join her husband. The young Tsar approached them, and addressing his conversation principally to the old courtier, told him what he had seen in his dream and what doubts the dream had left in his mind.

"That is a noble idea. It proves the rare nobility of your spirit," said the old man. "But forgive me for speaking frankly—you are too kind to be an emperor, and you exaggerate your responsibility. In the first place, the state of things is not as you imagine it to be. The people are not poor. They are well-to-do. Those who are poor are poor through their own fault. Only the guilty are punished, and if an unavoidable mistake does sometimes occur, it is like a thunderbolt—an accident, or the will of God. You have but one responsibility: to fulfill your task courageously and to retain the power that is given to you. You wish the best for your people and God sees that. As for the errors which you have committed unwittingly, you can pray for forgiveness, and God will guide you and pardon you. All the more because you have done nothing that demands forgiveness, and there never have been and never will be men possessed of such extraordinary qualities as you and your father. Therefore all we implore you to do is to live, and to reward our endless devotion and love with your favor, and everyone, save scoundrels who deserve no happiness, will be happy."

"What do you think about that?" the young Tsar asked his wife.

"I have a different opinion," said the clever young woman, who had been brought up in a free country. "I am glad you had that dream, and I agree with you that there are grave responsibilities resting upon you. I have often thought about it with great anxiety, and I think there is a simple means of casting off a part of the responsibility you are unable to bear, if not all of it. A large proportion of the power which is too heavy for you, you should delegate to the people, to its representatives, reserving for yourself only the supreme control, that is, the general direction of the affairs of State."

The Tsarina had hardly ceased to expound her views, when the old courtier began eagerly to refute her arguments, and they started a polite but very heated discussion.

For a time the young Tsar followed their arguments, but presently he ceased to be aware of what they said, listening only to the voice of him who had been his companion in the dream, and who was now speaking audibly in his heart.

"You are not only the Tsar," said the voice, "but more. You are a human being, who only yesterday came into this world, and will perchance tomorrow depart out of it. Apart from your duties as a Tsar, of which that old man is now speaking, you have more immediate duties not by any means to be disregarded—human duties, not the duties of a Tsar towards his subjects, which are only accidental, but an eternal duty, the duty of a man in his relation to God, the duty toward your own soul, which is to save it, and also, to serve God in establishing his kingdom on earth. You are not to be guarded in your actions either by what has been or what will be, but only by what it is your own duty to do."

He opened his eyes—his wife was awakening him. Which of the three courses the young Tsar chose, will be told in fifty years.

1894

MAKAR'S DREAM

Vladimir Korolenko

I

This is the tale of the dream that poor Makar who dwelt in a harsh and rigorous clime dreamt—the very Makar who is proverbial for his poor luck.

His birthplace was the out-of-the-way village of Chalgan lost in the wild taiga of Yakutia. Makar's fathers and grandfathers had wrested from the taiga a small piece of frozen ground. And although a hostile wall of dense dark woods surrounded it, they did not lose heart. Soon fences were running across the cleared land, ricks and stacks dotting it, and small smoking yurts growing fast on it; finally, on a hill, in the middle of the settlement, like a victory signal, a church steeple shot up into the sky. By and by Chalgan became a big village.

But in the course of the war they waged against the taiga, scorching it with fire, and attacking it with iron, Makar's fathers and grandfathers, almost without knowing it, became themselves a rude part of it. They married Yakut women, and adopted the language and customs of their wives, their own features of the Russian race to which they belonged becoming obliterated and fading altogether with time.

Be that as it may, my Makar remembered well that he came of the early Chalgan peasant stock. It was the place where he was born, where he lived and where he was destined to die. He was exceedingly proud of his lineage, and would now and then call others "foul Yakuts," though, to tell the truth, he himself was in no way different from the Yakuts in the ways and habits of his life. His Russian was poor, and he spoke it seldom; he dressed in animal skins, wore the short native deer hide boots, ate a single flat cake with a brew of tea brick on ordinary days, and on holidays and special occasions consumed as big a pot of drippings as was put before him on the table. He was extremely adept at riding on the back of a deer, and when he fell ill, he would call the medicine man; the latter, gritting his teeth fearsomely, would hurl himself in a frenzy on the sick man to scare off and expel from his body the illness which had settled there.

Makar slaved, lived in poverty, suffered hunger and cold. But did he have any other thoughts except the constant worry to earn his bread and tea?

Indeed, he had them.

When he was drunk, he wept and bemoaned his lot: "My God, what a life!" Besides, he kept saying that he would get away from everything and go up to the mountain. There he would not work the land or sow, neither cut nor cart wood; nor would he even grind grain by hand on the millstone. He would try only to save his soul. He did not know what the mountain was like, nor where it was; but he was certain it existed, for one thing, and for another, that it was far away, far enough for him to be out of the reach of the district police chief himself, the *ispravnik* ... And, of course, he would not have to pay any taxes ...

When sober he dropped the idea—perhaps because he saw the impossibility of finding such a marvelous mountain; but when drunk he grew bolder in his belief. He admitted, however, that he might not reach the right mountain and land on the wrong one. "I'd be lost then," he said. And yet he was determined to go to the mountain one day; if he had not carried out his intention, in all likelihood, it was due to the Tatars selling him poor vodka, which was hopped up with coarse tobacco for added strength, and which quickly sapped him of his vigor and made him ill.

II

It was Christmas Eve. Makar remembered that the following day was a great holiday. And he was overcome by an intense craving for vodka, but he had no money to buy it with. The corn was nearly all gone, and he was already in debt with the local shopkeepers and the Tatars. All the same tomorrow was the great holiday, on which he should not work—so what could he do if he did not get drunk? He felt wretched. What a life! There was the greatest feast day in the whole winter—and he not able to drink a bottle of vodka!

A happy thought struck him. He rose and began to pull on his ragged fur coat. His wife, who was a tall, wiry, remarkably strong and equally ugly woman, wise to all his tricks, guessed his intention at once.

"Where are you off to, you devil? Going to drink vodka by yourself?"

"Hold your tongue! I'm off to buy a bottle and we'll drink it tomorrow." He gave her a slap on the shoulder which nearly threw her off her balance, and winked slyly. Such is the heart of woman: she knew Makar would cheat her, and yet was taken in by her spouse's caress.

He went outdoors, found his old horse in the clearing, led it by its mane to the sleigh, and got it into harness. Soon the horse took its master out of the gate, stopped, turned its head and cast a questioning look at Makar who was lost in thought. Whereupon Makar gave the left rein a tug, directing the horse toward the outskirts of the village.

A small yurt stood at the very end of the village. A pillar of smoke, rising from it as from the other chimneys, hid the cold glittering stars and the bright moon behind a white billowing mantle. The firelight from within shone through the blocks of ice which served as windows. It was very quiet outdoors.

In this yurt dwelt strangers from afar. Makar did not know what ill luck had brought them to this distant wilderness, nor did he care in the least. He liked to do a little job for them now and then because they were not exacting and did not haggle about the pay.

Makar entered the yurt, walked straight up to the hearth, and stretched his hands which were numb with frost close to it.

"Tcha!" he ejaculated to inform them that he was cold.

The strangers were at home. A candle burned on the table, wastefully it seemed, for the strangers were not engaged in any work. One of them was lying on his bed, smoking and pensively eyeing the rings of blue smoke as they curled into the air, perhaps following some train of thought. The other was seated by the fireplace, in thought, too, watching the flames lick the burning logs.

"Hello!" said Makar, eager to break the uncomfortable silence.

Needless to say, he knew nothing of the sorrows that weighed heavily on the hearts of the strangers, nothing of the memories that haunted them on that very night, of the pictures brought into their mind by the flick of firelight and the smoke. Makar had his own big worry.

The young man sitting by the fire raised his head, and stared at Makar rather blankly as though he had not recognized him. Then he shook his head as though to clear it, and rose quickly from his chair.

"Oh, it's you, Makar! Hello! It's good to see you. Will you have a glass of tea with us?"

The offer pleased Makar.

"Tea?" he repeated inquiringly. "That's very good! ... Real good! Capital!"

He began briskly to take off his things. When he had laid aside his cap and coat, he felt far more at home, and the sight of the samovar with the glowing coals made him turn to the young man with a burst of warm feeling:

"I'm fond of you! It is the truth! So fond of you, so very much! I can't sleep at night for thought of you!"

The stranger turned around with a wry smile on his face.

"You're fond of us, you say?" he said. "Then what is it you want?"

Makar hesitated.

"I do have something in mind," he replied. "But how could you guess? Well, I'll tell you about it after I've had my tea."

Seeing that his hosts had offered him the tea of their own accord, Makar thought he might press things further.

"Any roast meat? I love it," he said.

"No."

"Never mind," said Makar reassuringly. "I'll take it some other time," and added, "some other time, eh?"

"All right."

Makar now took it for granted that the strangers owed him the roast meat, and he never forgot debts of this kind.

An hour later he was sitting in his sleigh, having earned a whole ruble by selling five prospective cartloads of firewood on quite satisfactory terms. True, he had promised solemnly not to spend the money on drink on that same day, knowing he would do just that. The pleasure he anticipated stilled any pricks of conscience he might have, and he did not even give a thought to the beating he would be sure to get from his faithful wife when he returned home drunk, having deceived her.

"Where's that you're going, Makar?" one of the strangers called out laughingly when he saw Makar's horse, instead of going straïght on, turning to the left, to the Tatars' establishment.

"Whoa! Did you ever see such a wretched horse? Where are you going?" Makar shouted, blaming the horse, tugging hard at the left rein, and giving the animal furtive little slaps with the right.

The clever beast whisked its tail reproachfully, and trotted quietly in the needed direction. And then the squeak of the runners abruptly ceased at the door of the Tatar pub.

III

Near that gate there stood several tethered horses with the high Yakut saddles. In the small hut the air was suffocating. Acrid fumes of poor tobacco formed a thick haze and were slowly blown out into the chimney. Visiting Yakuts sat on benches behind tables on which stood mugs of vodka; here and there were groups of men playing cards. The customers' faces were flushed and streaming with perspiration. The eyes of the players were wildly intent on their cards. Money flashed quickly from one player's pocket into another's. In one corner of the room a drunken Yakut sat on a bundle of straw rocking himself to-and-fro and singing. In shrill, grating notes, he repeated in a variety of tunes that tomorrow was a great holiday and that today he was drunk.

Makar put down his money and a bottle was handed to him. He tucked it into his bosom and retired unperceived into a dark corner. Pouring himself out one glassful after another, he swilled the vodka greedily. It was very bitter; it had been mixed three quarters with water owing to the holiday, but the tobacco had been put in freely. After each gulp Makar gasped for breath and saw red rings dancing before his eyes.

He was soon drunk, and he, too, sank down on the straw, locked his arms around his knees and laid his heavy head on them. In this position, he began to produce strange shrill sounds, singing the song that tomorrow was a great holiday and that he had drunk five firewood loads' worth of drink.

Meanwhile the hut was getting more and more crammed with customers. The Yakuts who had come to attend the church service and drink the Tatar vodka kept pouring in. Seeing that in a short while there might be no more room for newcomers, the keeper stood up and took a good look around him. His eye fell on the Yakut and on Makar in the dark corner.

Whereupon he walked over to the Yakut, grabbed him by the collar of his coat and flung him out of the hut. Then came Makar's turn. As he was a local inhabitant, the Tatar keeper accorded him a greater honor: he opened the door wide and gave him such a hearty kick that Makar flew out of the hut and fell on his nose upon a mound of snow.

It is hard to say if he felt affronted by such treatment. The snow stuck to his face and penetrated inside his sleeves. With difficulty he dragged himself up from the snow and staggered toward his sledge.

The moon had risen high overhead. The tail of the Big Dipper pointed downward. It was getting frostier. In the north, from behind a hemispheric dark cloud appeared the first fiery flashes of the northern lights.

Aware apparently of its master's state, the horse slowly and prudently wended its way home. Makar sat upon the sledge, rocking himself and singing the same song. He sang that he had drunk five fuel loads' worth of vodka and that his old lady would give him a beating. The sounds that escaped from his throat shrilled and moaned through the evening air. And there was something so doleful and plaintive about Makar's singing that the stranger who had climbed on top of the yurt to shut the chimney felt even more heavy of heart. Meanwhile the horse had brought the sleigh up to a hilltop from which the country around opened to view. The snow sparkled in the moonlight, but when the light of the moon seemed to fade, the snow grew shadowy and shimmered faintly with the reflected glow of the northern lights. And in that shifting glow the snow-covered hills and the forest on them seemed now to crowd in upon Makar, now to recede far into the distance. Makar thought he saw distinctly the snowy bald patch of Yamalakh Hill on the other side of which he had set traps for animals and birds.

This launched him on a new train of thought, and he sang joyfully that a fox had been caught in his trap. He would sell the skin the next day and thus escape a beating from his wife.

The bells started to ring when Makar entered his hut, and he at once told his wife that a fox had been caught in his trap. He had quite forgotten that his wife had not shared his bottle, and therefore when she landed him a heavy blow in the small of his back in answer to the joyful tidings, it took him by surprise. And before he had time to throw himself on the bed, she cuffed his neck.

Meanwhile the bells were ringing for the midnight mass in Chalgan, their sounds floating far away in the air, across the snows.

IV

He was lying on his bed. His head was burning and a fire seemed to be raging inside him. The mixture of vodka and tobacco was like a liquid fire coursing through his veins. Melting snow ran down his face and back in ice-cold streamlets.

His old woman thought he was asleep, but he was awake, and could not get the fox out of his mind. He was now quite sure it had been trapped, even knew in which gin it was caught. He could see it distinctly—kept under by the heavy block, tearing at the hard snow with its claws and trying to escape. Moonbeams streaming through the thick underwood gleamed on its golden fur. And the animal's eyes glowed with a beckoning glint in them.

The vision was too much for him. He rose from the bed and directed his steps toward his faithful horse to drive to the taiga.

What was that? Did his wife grab him by the collar of his coat and was she pulling him back?

No, he has left the village behind him. He could hear the even crack of the snow beneath the runners of the sleigh. He has left Chalgan far behind. The bells were still ringing solemnly. And he could see rows of riders sharply silhouetted with their high peaked hats against the dark line of the horizon. They were Yakuts on their way to church.

Meanwhile the moon sank lower in the sky, while way in the zenith a whitish cloud appeared and shone with a phosphorescent light. The cloud expanded and then suddenly burst with flashes of bright color spreading on all sides. These flashes leaped across a hemispheric dark cloud in the north which from the contrasting brightness looked even blacker. It became blacker than the taiga toward which Makar was now making his way.

The road wound between low shrubs, with hills on the left and the right. As he drove on, the trees grew taller, and the undergrowth thicker. The taiga was silent and full of mystery. Silvery hoarfrost rested on the bare branches of the larches. But as the soft glow of the northern lights threaded its way from the treetops to the ground below there would suddenly flash into view a snowbound glade, or, beneath the snow-drifts, the huge skeletons of fallen woodland giants ... Then darkness again, utter silence, and the spell of mystery.

Makar stopped his horse. He had reached the spot, quite close to the road, where all the traps were laid. In the phosphorescent light he could see distinctly the low wattle fence, and even the first trap. It was made up of three heavy beams resting on a slightly slanting pole, all held together by a clever contraption of levers and horsehair cord.

Now, this was another man's gin; what if the fox had gone into it? Makar climbed quickly out of his sledge, left his smart little horse standing on the road, and listened.

There was not a sound, except for the solemn chiming of the bells coming from the village, which was now far away and out of sight.

He had nothing to fear. The man to whom the traps belonged, Alyoshka of Chalgan, who was Makar's neighbor and sworn enemy, was probably in church. Not a single print was to be seen on the smooth surface of the freshly fallen snow. Makar walked around the traps, the snow crunching beneath his tread. The traps were wide open, waiting with gaping maws for their prey. He went back and forth—nothing; he retraced his steps to the road.

Pst! … pst! There was a faint rustling. A fox! Its fur gleamed red in the moonlight so close to Makar that he could see the sharp-pointed ears, and with a whisk of the bushy tail the fox seemed to entice him farther into the thicket. The animal now vanished between the trees in the direction of Makar's own traps. And a dull thud soon rang through the woods setting off a broken muffled echo which died down in a far off gulley.

Makar's heart began to pound: the trap had closed.

He broke into a run, making his way through the undergrowth. The cold twigs struck him in the eyes, powdering his face with snow. He stumbled and gasped for breath.

Presently he reached a clearing which he had made himself. On two sides of it stood trees white with hoarfrost, and farther down, tapering, ran a path at the end of which was the opening of a trap eagerly awaiting its prey … He was now close to the spot …

But what did he see? The flicker of a figure on the path near his traps. He recognized Alyoshka—it was his short squat figure, his sloping shoulders, and his clumsy bear's gait. Makar thought that Alyoshka's swarthy face had grown even darker and his grin was wider than usual.

Makar felt deeply outraged. "The scoundrel! He is after my gins." To be sure, Makar had just been himself around Alyoshka's traps. But there was a difference.

When prowling about others' traps he feared to be caught, whereas when others trespassed on his ground he was resentful and was most eager to lay his hands on the offender.

And he ran now quickly toward the trap in which the fox had been captured. Alyoshka shuffled with his bear's gait in the same direction. Makar knew that he needed to get there first.

There was the trap with the block down. And from under it he caught a glimpse of the trapped fox's red fur. The fox was tearing up the hard snow with its claws just as he had imagined it would be doing and glared at him with its sharp burning eyes.

"*Tytyma!*" shouted Makar in Yakut. "Don't touch it! It's mine."

"Tytyma!" retorted Alyoshka, like an echo. "It's mine."

Both men reached the trap at the same time and, jostling each other, began lifting the trapping block to get at the fox. As the block came up the animal leaped forward; then it paused, cast a somewhat disdainful look at both men, licked the spot which had been bruised by the block, and ran merrily off with a whisk of its tail.

Just as Alyoshka was going to make off after it, Makar caught hold of the tails of his coat.

"Tytyma!" he shouted. "It's mine!" And he hurried after the fox himself.

"Tytyma!" repeated Alyoshka, his voice again ringing echo-like. Makar felt his own coat tails being dragged back and the next moment Alyoshka was running in front.

Makar grew angry. And forgetting about the fox he dashed after Alyoshka. Faster and faster they ran. Alyoshka's cap was torn from his head by the tree branches, but he did not stop to pick it up, because Makar, shrieking angrily, was close on his heels. However, Alyoshka was far more cunning than poor Makar. Suddenly he stopped, turned, and bent down his head, which hit the running Makar below the waist and he tumbled down into the snow. And as he fell, the wily Alyoshka snatched the fur cap off his head and disappeared in the taiga.

Makar rose slowly, feeling miserable and outwitted. He could not be in a more wretched frame of mind. To think that the fox had practically been his and now it was gone … He thought he saw the mocking flick of its tail in the darkness as it scurried away for good.

It grew darker still, and there was only a tiny bit of the whitish cloud visible high above. From its fading glow there spread wearily and languidly the last dying flashes of the northern lights.

Cold-stinging streamlets of melted snow trickled down Makar's hot body. The snow had penetrated inside his sleeves, his collar, and into his boots. The accursed Alyoshka had carried off his cap. He had lost his mitts. Things looked bad for him. He knew only too well that it was no joke to be out on such a frosty night in the taiga without a cap or mitts.

He had been walking toward home for some time now, but the way seemed endless. He figured he should have been out of the Yamalakh Hill grounds and in sight of the church steeple. From afar came the ringing of the church bells, and though he thought he was approaching the sound, it became even fainter.

Makar's heart sank and despair gripped him.

He was weary and miserable. His legs refused to carry him, his whole body ached. He gasped for breath. His feet and hands were numb with cold. And his hatless head felt as though it were locked in a vice of red-hot steel.

"It looks like I'm lost," the thought throbbed in his head, but he trudged on.

The taiga was still. With a stubborn hostility the trees closed in on him, with no light anywhere in between them, no hope.

"I'm lost!" the thought persisted.

He felt very faint. Shamelessly the tree branches now lashed him in the face, mocking at his helplessness. A white hare ran across a clearing, sat down on its haunches, moved its black-dotted long ears, and began to wash itself, making faces at Makar. The hare meant to say that he knew Makar well enough, that he was the very Makar who had set traps in the taiga to catch it, and that now it was good to see him having fallen into a trap himself.

Makar's despair grew. Meanwhile the taiga was coming alive—with hostility. Even faraway trees now stretched out long branches to catch him by the hair and lash him across the eyes and face. The grouse came out of their holes and stared at him with their curious round eyes, and the woodcocks hopped about between them with outspread wings, chattering loudly, and telling their wives about him and his tricks. Thousands of foxes peeped out of the thicket, sniffing the air, moving their sharp-pointed ears, and eyeing Makar scornfully. The hares sat on their haunches and gleefully informed one another that he had got lost in the taiga.

It was all too much for Makar to bear.

"I am lost!" thought Makar and there and then he made up his mind to get on with it.

He lay down on the snow.

It had become colder. The last flashes of the aurora glowed faintly in the sky, peeping at Makar from between the treetops. A soft treble of the church bells came floating softly through the air from Chalgan.

The aurora shimmered and faded away. The sounds ceased. And Makar was dead.

V

He was not aware of just how it happened. He knew only that something ought to go out of him; he was expecting it to go out, yet it did not.

Meanwhile he knew that he was dead, and he lay there meekly, quite motionless. He remained motionless so long that he grew tired of it.

It was quite dark when Makar felt someone kick him. He turned his head and opened his eyes.

The larches stood high above him humble and still; they looked ashamed of the pranks they had been playing on him. The shaggy fir-trees stretched out their big, snow-covered arms and rocked softly. And sparkling little snowflakes floated just as softly through the air.

From between the many branches, the bright, kind stars peeped out of the sky. And they seemed to say: "Alas, the poor man is dead."

Over Makar's body stood the old priest Ivan, kicking him with his foot. The priest's long robe was powdered with snow; snow glistened on his fur cap, his shoulders, and long beard. Most astonishing it was that the man should be the very priest Ivan who had died four years ago.

He had been a kindhearted churchman, not troubling Makar too much about the tithes and fees. Makar himself settled the fees for christenings and masses. And he now recalled with a pang of shame that he had been quite closefisted and stingy, paying the smallest fee and at times nothing at all. The priest Ivan did not take offense; the one thing he insisted on was that he get his bottle of vodka. Moreover, if Makar did not have the money to buy the spirits, the priest Ivan would send for it, and share the bottle with him. At such times the priest would generally become dead drunk, but he would rarely fight, and not too hard if he would. In this state, helpless and defenseless, Makar would deliver him into the tender care of his wife.

Yes, he had been a kindly little priest, but he met with a bad death. One day when everybody left the house, and he was lying alone drunk on his bed, he hankered for a smoke. And so he rose from his bed, reeled over to the fireplace to light his pipe, lost his balance, and fell into the fire. When his family returned, there was nothing left of Father Ivan but his legs.

All the parishioners mourned for the good priest Ivan, but as all that remained were his legs, there was no doctor who could help. And it was his legs that were buried; and another priest came in his place.

To think that it was the same Father Ivan who was now standing over Makar, whole, and kicking him lightly with his foot.

"Get up, Makar, my friend!" he was saying. "Come along with me."

"Where to?" asked Makar sulkily.

Being lost and dead he had only to lie still, and was no longer obliged to wander through the pathless taiga. Otherwise, what would have been the point in getting lost?

"We'll go to the Great *Toyon*!"

"And why should I go to him?" asked Makar.

"To be judged," said the priest sadly, and in a somewhat sentimental tone of voice.

Makar remembered that indeed after death one is supposed to appear somewhere at a judgment. He had heard it in church. The priest was right; there was no help for it, and he would have to get up.

And so he rose, grumbling that there was no rest for a body even after death.

The little priest went on ahead and Makar followed him. They kept a straight path. The larches humbly moved aside to give them way, as they went eastwards.

Makar noticed with astonishment that the priest left no footprints behind him. Looking down at his own feet, he saw that there were no traces of his footsteps either; the snow remained perfectly smooth and unfurrowed.

It occurred to him what an advantage this would be, for then he could prowl about undetected around other people's traps, when the priest, who apparently had read his thoughts, turned sharply around and said:

"*Kabys!* Stop it! You do not know what every such thought may cost you."

"Of all things!" growled Makar. "Can't a body think what he likes? What's made you grow so strict all of a sudden? Who are you to talk?!"

The priest shook his head reprovingly and walked on.

"Have we far to go?" Makar asked.

"Very far," replied the other dolefully.

"But what shall we eat?" asked Makar worriedly.

"Have you forgotten that you are dead," retorted the priest, turning around, "and that you will no longer need food nor drink."

This was not to Makar's liking at all. This not needing food would be all right if there was no food anyhow, but then why wasn't he left in peace to lie in the snow? But to walk far without eating at all seemed to him a most unreasonable thing to do. And he started to grumble again.

"Do not grumble!" said the priest.

"Very well!" Makar retorted sulkily. But he went on grumbling in his heart and finding fault with everything. "Who ever heard of such a thing? They make a body walk on and on without a morsel to eat!"

He walked on behind the priest, nursing his grudges. They had walked for what seemed a very long time. And though Makar had not seen the dawn yet, it seemed to him that they had been on the road for a whole week or more. They had passed high-peaked mountains and ravines without number, and had left behind them many woods and glades, rivers and lakes. Whenever Makar looked around, the somber taiga seemed to be receding fast behind them, the high snow-covered mountains fading in the darkness and dipping fast beyond the horizon.

Their way seemed to lead higher and higher. The stars were shining brighter. And presently the setting moon peeped from behind the crest of the hill they were ascending. The moon seemed to be running away from them, but Makar and the priest were close behind it, until it again began to rise above the horizon. They were now walking on the top of a broad, flat plain.

It grew much lighter than it had been during the early part of the night. The reason for this, of course, was that they were much closer to the stars. The stars were as big as apples, and of dazzling brilliance, while the moon was the size of the bottom of a golden cask, and shone like the sun, illuminating the whole plain from end to end.

Each snowflake on the plain was visible. Many roads ran across the plain and all converged toward a single spot in the east. People of every description, dressed in all kinds of garb, were walking and riding along these roads.

After peering for some time at a man on horseback, Makar suddenly turned off the road and ran after him. "Stop! Stop!" shouted the priest, but Makar did not heed him. He had recognized in the rider a Tatar who had stolen his horse six years back, and had been dead for five years. There he was riding the selfsame skewbald horse, which galloped friskily, raising a cloud of snow, sparkling and scintillating with color in the starlight. Makar was astonished to see how easily and quickly he had overtaken on foot the fast-riding Tatar. The other had stopped his horse at once when he saw Makar come up to him. Makar flew at him in a rage.

"Come with me to the Elder!" he shouted. "The horse is mine! I know it by the slit in its right ear … Smart, aren't you? You ride another man's horse while its master walks like a beggar!"

"Wait a minute!" the Tatar responded. "There is no need to go to the Elder. It's your horse, you say? Take it back by all means. The confounded brute! This is the fifth year I've been riding it and I have not moved an inch … People who go on foot keep leaving me behind—which is a shame for an honest Tatar!"

He had raised his leg to get down from the saddle when the priest came running up panting for breath and dragged Makar away.

"You wretch! What are you doing? Can't you see that the Tatar wants to cheat you?"

"To be sure, he's cheating me!" Makar cried gesticulating angrily. "The horse was as good as any, a real fine horse. They offered me forty rubles for it when it was three years old … No, fellow, you won't get away with this, if you've spoiled the horse, I shall kill it for the meat, and you will pay me cash. D'you think you are going to be let off just because you are a Tatar?"

Makar had been working himself up into a fury and shouting on purpose; he was trying to attract a crowd as he had a fear of Tatars. At this point the priest intervened.

"Hush, Makar, hush!" he said. "Have you forgotten that you are dead? What good will the horse do you now? Can't you see you are moving far quicker on foot than the Tatar on horseback? How would you like it if you had to ride for a thousand years?"

Makar now guessed why the Tatar had been so eager to return the horse.

"They are shrewd folk!" he thought and turned to the Tatar.

"Very well," he said. "Go ahead and ride, but I intend to go to the law about this business, my fellow."

The Tatar pulled down his cap angrily over his eyes, and whipped the horse. The animal pranced up; snow flew up from its hoofs, but it advanced not a step until Makar and the priest started to move.

The Tatar spat out angrily and, turning to Makar, said: "Look here, *dogor*, my friend, have you a little tobacco to spare? I am dying for a smoke, and I ran out of my own tobacco four years back."

"A dog is your friend, not me!" Makar retorted angrily. "See here, he's stolen my horse and now he asks for my tobacco. I don't care if the devil takes you, not a bit."

With these words Makar walked off on his own way.

"You were wrong to deny him a small leaf of tobacco," said Father Ivan. "If you had been kinder, the Toyon would have forgiven you no less than a hundred sins."

"Why hadn't you told that to me before?" Makar snapped.

"It's too late to teach you now what you ought to have learned from your priests in your lifetime."

He was enraged. What was the use of having priests? You pay your tithes, and they cannot even instruct you when to let a Tatar have a leaf of tobacco in order to receive forgiveness for your sins. It was no joke ... one hundred sins ... all for one leaf! To be sure, that was a good bargain!

"Hold on!" he exclaimed. "One leaf will do for us, and I will give four to the Tatar. That will make four hundred sins!"

"Look behind you!" the priest said.

Makar obeyed. Behind them stretched the boundless snowy plain. The Tatar now looked like a mere speck, Makar thought he saw the white dust rise from under the hoofs of his skewbald horse, but presently even that little speck vanished from view.

"Oh, well," Makar remarked, "he'll manage without my tobacco. Look at the way he's ruined the horse, the accursed man!"

"No," said the priest, "he has not ruined the horse but he stole it. Do you not remember the old men saying that you cannot ride far on a stolen horse?"

Makar indeed remembered the old men saying so, but as he had frequently seen during his life that the Tatars rode to town on stolen horses he had not put much faith in their words. Now however, he realized that the old men could speak the truth.

He passed many riders on the plain. They all rode at the same speed as the first. The horses galloped with bird-like speed, the riders strained and sweated. And yet Makar kept overtaking them and leaving them far behind.

Most of the riders were Tatars, but quite a few were natives of Chalgan. Some of the latter were riding oxen which they had most likely stolen and urged them on with goads.

Makar cast looks of hate at the Tatars and each time he passed one, it was with the remark that it served him right. But with the men from Chalgan he stopped to chat good-humoredly; for them he felt a kinship though they were thieves. He went even so far as to assist them to drive the animals with a switch he picked up on the way, but the men who were riding always fell behind, and soon faded away into mere specks.

The plain seemed boundless. Despite the many persons on horseback and on foot that they kept leaving behind, the plain appeared to be deserted. Hundreds— perhaps thousands—of versts seemed to lie between every one or two travellers.

Among other persons, Makar met an old man he could not recognize, although his face, garb, and even his gait seemed to indicate that he was a native of Chalgan. But Makar could not remember ever having met him before. The old fellow wore a threadbare coat, old leather breeches, and torn top boots made of calfskin. He seemed very old, and what was stranger still, he carried on his back an even more ancient old woman whose feet dragged on the ground. The poor old fellow gasped for breath, stumbled under his burden, and leaned heavily on his staff. Makar felt sorry for him. He halted, and so did the old man.

"*Kapse*," said Makar cordially. Speak.

"I've nothing to say," returned the old man.

"What have you heard?"

"Nothing."

"What have you seen?"

"I've seen nothing."

Makar held his tongue for a while, after which he deemed it right to ask the old man who he was and where he was bound.

After giving his name, the old man told him that many years ago, how many he did not know himself, he had abandoned the village of Chalgan and gone to live on the mountain to save his soul. There he never did a stitch of work, lived on berries and roots, neither ploughed nor sowed, nor ground the corn, nor did he pay any taxes. When he died and appeared before the Toyon for judgment, the latter asked him who he was, and what he had been doing. He replied that he lived on the mountain to gain his salvation. "Very well," said the Toyon, "but where is your old woman? Go and fetch her." Off he went to fetch her only to find that his old woman had turned into a beggar. There had been no one to provide for her. She had neither house, nor cows, nor bread, and had grown so weak that her legs wouldn't keep her. And so he was obliged to drag her on his back to the Toyon.

The old man started to weep, but the old woman kicked him as if he had been a beast of burden, and said in a feeble, cross voice:

"Go on!"

This made Makar feel even sorrier for the old man, and he was glad that he had never gone up on that mountain. Had he gone he would have fared even worse, because his own wife, a hefty and tall woman, was hard to carry. And were she to kick him as if he were an ox, she would soon drive him to a second death.

Out of pity for him, Makar tried to help the old man by holding up the woman's legs, but he was compelled to let go of them after a few steps for fear of tearing her feet off. And then in the twinkling of an eye the old man vanished with his burden.

As they went on, Makar met no other persons worthy of his attention. They passed thieves, loaded with stolen goods like beasts of burden, and crawling along at a snail's pace; fat Yakut chiefs sat rocking on their high saddles, their tall hats reaching into the clouds like spires and by their side trotted and hopped poor workers, lean and light-footed like hares. A sullen, gory murderer slunk past them with roving eyes. In vain he thrust himself into the snow to wash off the bloodstains! The snow immediately turned dark red, while the stains on the slayer stood out more distinctly; there was now wild despair and horror in his look. But he pressed on avoiding the terrified glances of other wayfarers.

The souls of little children hovered in the air like tiny birdies. There were big flocks of them, and no wonder! The coarse food, squalor, the open hearths, and the icy draughts of the yurts took a toll on them by the hundreds in Chalgan alone. When they caught up with the murderer, they shied away in a whole flock, quite panic-stricken, and long afterward the rustling of their little wings could be heard in the air.

Makar could not help noting that he moved with considerable speed compared with other travellers, and he lost no time in ascribing this fact to his own goodness.

"Look here, *agabyt*," he said to the priest. "I may have been a little too fond of the bottle in my time, but after all I was a good man … What do you think? I believe God loves me."

He eyed the priest closely, wondering whether he could draw him out concerning certain things. But the priest merely said:

"Do not be proud. We'll soon be there, where you will learn for yourself."

Just then Makar noticed that it was less dark in the plain and that it must be dawning. A few rays rose from behind the horizon and they drifted across the sky, extinguishing the bright stars. The moon, too, was blotted out like the stars. The snowbound plain lay wrapped in shadow.

Mists now rose on all sides of the plain, arrayed like a guard of honor.

At one point, in the east, the mists grew lighter and were clad in gold, like warriors.

Then the mists swayed, and the golden warriors bent low.

From behind them the sun rose, settled upon the gilt mountain ridges and beamed upon the plain, flooding it with its dazzling brilliance. And the mists now soared triumphantly in a glorious ring, broke up in the west and, fluttering, drifted off into the heights above.

Makar thought that he heard a marvelous song. It was the very hymn with which the earth greeted the rising sun every day. Only Makar had not paid attention to it before, and this was the first time in all his life that he realized how beautiful the song was.

He stood still listening to it, and refused to go any farther. He could stand there forever listening to it …

Father Ivan touched his arm.

"Let us go in," he said. "We have arrived!"

Only then did Makar behold a great big door which had been concealed by the mists.

He was extremely loath to enter through the door, but there was no backing out—and he obeyed the summons.

VI

They entered a well-appointed, roomy house, and only when he was indoors did Makar realize how frosty it was outside. In the middle of the house was a beautifully adorned hearth. It was made of pure silver, and in it burned a few golden logs which gave off a pleasant warmth that went right through your whole body. The eyes did not smart from the flame of this marvelous hearth, nor did it scorch the skin. It merely made one feel so agreeably warm that Makar would have liked to stand there warming himself forever. Father Ivan walked up to the hearth and held his hands, numb with cold, toward the fire.

The house had four doors, one was the front door through which they had entered, and the three others seemed to lead to inner rooms. Young men in long white shirts were going in and out of these doors. Makar thought they might be persons working for the Toyon. Vaguely he remembered having seen them somewhere, but he could not remember precisely where. Wonderingly he noted that each of them had two large white wings attached to his back, and it occurred to Makar that the Toyon must have other workers besides these, for it was impossible to pass into the thick forest to fell wood with such a pair of wings.

One of the men walked up to the hearth and, turning his back to the fire, struck up a conversation with Father Ivan.

"Speak!"

"I have nothing to say," replied the priest.

"What news is there in the world?"

"I have heard nothing."

"What did you see?"

"Nothing."

After both were silent for a short while, the priest remarked: "I have brought a man with me."

"From Chalgan?"

"Yes, he comes from Chalgan."

"In that case I must fetch the big scales."

He walked out of one door, while Makar asked the priest what the scales were needed for and why they must be big ones.

"You see," the priest began, a little embarrassed, "the scales are needed to weigh the good and the evil you have done in your life. Where most persons are concerned the good and bad actions weigh about the same, but the inhabitants of Chalgan are so sinful that the Toyon ordered special scales to be made for them with a huge balance for weighing their sins."

These words made Makar's heart quail. And his courage faltered.

The serving men reappeared carrying a huge balance. One scale was of gold and very small, the other was of wood and extremely large. Under the latter yawned a great big hole.

Makar went up to see if the scales were in order, examining them closely. There appeared to be nothing tricky about them. Both scales were on a level, neither outbalancing the other.

He did not quite understand just how the balance was arranged, and would have preferred the familiar steelyard balance he had used all his life, and which he knew, when buying or selling, how to turn in his favor.

"The Toyon comes!" said Father Ivan, smoothing his robe.

The middle door opened and the Toyon entered. He was a very ancient man, with a flowing silvery beard that reached to his waist. He was clad in rich furs and fabrics such as Makar had never seen, and wore warm boots trimmed with plush, which Makar remembered having seen an old icon-painter wear.

His very first glance at the old Toyon told Makar that he was the same old man Makar had seen painted on the church walls. Only he was now without his son, who was most likely away on some household business of his own. A dove flew into the room and, after fluttering for some time, perched on his knee. The old Toyon took to stroking the bird as he seated himself on a chair which had been prepared for him.

The old Toyon had a kind face, and when Makar felt his heart grow heavy, he looked at that face and drew comfort from it.

His heart had grown heavy because he had suddenly remembered his whole life down to the smallest details, remembering each step of it, each stroke of the axe, each tree he had felled, each deception he had practiced, and each glass of vodka he had drunk.

He felt ashamed and frightened. But one glance at the old Toyon's face gave him new courage. And once he felt this new courage, he hoped to be able to conceal some of his bad deeds.

The old Toyon now eyed him and asked who he was, whence he came, what his name and age were.

After Makar had answered the questions, the old Toyon asked: "For what deeds can you account in your life?"

"You know them yourself," retorted Makar. "I dare say, you've got them all recorded."

These words were only a trick Makar used to find out from the Toyon if everything was indeed written down.

"Speak up yourself," replied the old Toyon.

Makar brightened up again.

He started off by enumerating every kind of work he had done, and though he remembered well every blow of the axe he had struck, every branch he had cut down, and each furrow he had made with the plough, he added on thousands of bundles of kindle, hundreds of cartloads of wood, and hundreds of pounds of corn sowed.

When he had completed his account, the old Toyon told the priest Ivan to fetch the book.

It then dawned on Makar that the priest was the old Toyon's secretary. This angered him greatly because the priest had dropped no hint about this to him.

Father Ivan now brought an enormous book, opened it, and began to read.

"Look up the number of kindle bundles," said the old Toyon.

The priest looked them up and said sadly:

"He has added as many as thirteen thousand bundles."

"He's lying," Makar shouted truculently. "He can't count right for he's been a drunkard and died an ugly death."

"You had better hold your tongue!" said the old Toyon. "Did he charge you unfairly for your weddings or your christenings? Did he extort tithes from you?"

"I won't say he did," replied Makar.

"There you see!" said the old Toyon. "As to his fondness for drink, I know of it." The old Toyon was truly angry.

"Read his sins as they are put down in the book," he said. "I no longer trust him, for he is a liar."

Meanwhile the underlings had dropped onto the golden scale the bundles, and the wood, the plowing—in short, all the labor he had done. There was such a big amount that the golden scale went down, while the wooden one rose so very high that God's young serving men could not reach up to it with their hands and were obliged to fly up and no less than a hundred of them were pulling it down by the rope.

The labor of this man from Chalgan was heavy indeed!

Father Ivan began reading. He started with cheating, of which there were 21,933 instances. Next the priest proceeded to count the bottles of vodka Makar had drunk—they amounted to four hundred. And as the priest read, Makar saw the wooden scale go down and down, reaching to the pit below.

Aware of how bad things were for him, Makar thought he might improve them, and drawing near the scale he tried furtively to keep it up with his foot. But one of the servants caught him doing it and raised quite a row.

"What's happening there?" asked the old Toyon.

"He was going to support the scale with his foot," replied the servant. The Toyon turned crossly to Makar.

"I see that you are a cheat, a lazybones, and a drunkard! There are debts you have not paid, you owe the priest his tithes, and you have made the ispravnik sin by swearing at you!"

It was now to Father Ivan that the Toyon addressed himself.

"What man in all Chalgan," he asked, "lays the heaviest load on his horses and drives them the hardest?"

"The Elder of the church," replied Father Ivan. "He carries the mail, and drives the ispravnik, too."

The old Toyon then said:

"Send this lazy fellow to the Elder. He shall be one of his horses and draw the ispravnik till he can work no more … After that we shall see …"

The old Toyon had hardly finished talking when the door opened to let in his son who now seated himself at his right.

"I have heard your verdict," the son said. "I have lived long in the world and know the affairs of the world well. It will be hard on the unfortunate man to be harnessed to drive the ispravnik! But ... so be it! Yet perhaps he has something to say for himself. Speak, my poor fellow!"

A very astonishing thing now happened. The very Makar, who in all his life could not utter as many as ten words in a row, suddenly waxed eloquent. He himself marveled at the change in him. There now seemed to be two persons: a Makar who spoke, and a Makar who listened to his own words in amazement. He could not believe his ears. His speech flowed smoothly, and he spoke with ardor, one word followed another and then all the words lined up in long neat rows. He was not a bit shy. And if he happened to stumble, he at once regained his confidence and spoke twice as loud. And most important—he felt that his words carried conviction.

The old Toyon, who had been cross with him at first, now listened with growing attention, as though assured that Makar was not at all the fool he had appeared to be. At the beginning Father Ivan was aghast and tried to stop Makar by pulling him by the coattails, but Makar shook him off and went on speaking. Presently the priest was reassured and listened beamingly to his parishioner setting forth the truth. And he saw that the old Toyon was pleased, too, to hear the truth. Even the young serving men in their long shirts and with white wings who worked for the Toyon came from their quarters to the doors and listened wonderingly to Makar's speech, nudging one another as they drank in his words.

He began by saying that he had no desire to become a horse of the church Elder. And not because he feared the hard work but because the verdict was unfair. And since it was a wrong verdict, he was not going to obey it—not for anything in the world. Let them do with him what they please—he did not even care if he were given up to the devils. It was unfair to make him drive the ispravnik! Nor let them imagine that he feared to be a horse; for if the Elder overworked his horses he fed them with oats. And he, Makar, who had been overworked all his life, had never been fed oats.

"Who overworked you?" asked the old Toyon.

Who? Why, everybody, and all his life long. The village Elders, the foremen, the justices, and the ispravniki were always after him to pay his taxes and the priests to pay the tithes. Hunger and misery drove him hard; he had suffered from the drought in summer and the bitter frosts in winter; the taiga and the frozen soil yielded him nothing! His life had been like that of cattle that are being driven on and do not know where they are going. Did he know what the priest's sermons in church meant and why he had to pay the tithes? Did he know what had become of his eldest son, who had been taken as a soldier? He did not know where he died, or in what place his poor bones lay!

They said that he drank much vodka. That was true enough; his heart had ached for the vodka.

"How many bottles did you say?" Makar asked.

"Four hundred," replied the priest after consulting the book.

Very well! But was it real vodka? Three quarters of it was water, and one quarter was vodka in which tobacco had been infused to make it stronger. Therefore three hundred bottles may well be struck off his account.

"Is this true?" asked the old Toyon of the priest, and you could see the anger still smoldering in him.

"It is the truth indeed," Father Ivan replied hurriedly.

And Makar continued. He had added thirteen thousand bundles of kindling. That may be so! He had made only sixteen thousand. Was that not enough? And mind you, he had made two thousand when his first wife was lying ill. His heart ached, he longed to sit by his sick wife, but he was obliged to go to work in the taiga. And there he had wept, his tears freezing to his eyelashes, and the cold and the grief going to his very heart ... but he went on working.

Soon afterwards his wife died. And he had no money to give her proper burial. He hired himself out to cut wood so that he could pay for his wife's abode in the hereafter. Knowing what dire need he had of the money, the merchant who hired him paid only ten kopecks for each load ... And his dead wife was lying alone in the cold house, while he went on cutting wood and weeping bitterly. Surely these loads of wood were worth five times and even more of their value!

There were tears in the eyes of the old Toyon, and Makar now saw the scales waver: the wooden one went up while the golden sank.

Makar went on speaking. They had everything down in their books, they said. Would they then see if he had ever known affection, kindness, and joy. Where were his children? If they died young, he mourned and bewailed them, but those who grew up left him to struggle alone against need and poverty. He had grown old alone with his second wife, and had felt the strength failing him, and miserable old age creep upon him. They were alone, as alone as two lonely fir trees in the steppe, mercilessly exposed to the cruel snowstorms.

"Is that true?" the old Toyon asked once again. And the priest answered:

"It is perfectly true!"

The scales wavered again ... and the old Toyon lapsed into thought.

"How is this?" he said. "After all there are pure and just men living on the earth. Their eyes are clear, their faces are radiant, and their garments spotless. Their hearts are as tender as bounteous soil; they receive the good seed, and bring forth the beautiful, fragrant fruit and flowers, the perfume of which is sweet to me. And you? Look at yourself!"

All eyes were turned on Makar, and he felt ashamed. He knew that his eyes were dim, and his face was dark, his hair and beard were matted, and his clothes torn. He had been thinking of buying a pair of boots before his death, in order to appear at the judgment seat as behooves an upright peasant. But he had always spent the money on drink, and now he stood before the Toyon in ragged boots, like the worst of the Yakuts ... He felt utterly wretched.

"Your face is dark," the Toyon continued. "Your eyes are dim and your clothes are ragged. And your heart is overgrown with weeds and thorns, and wormwood. That is why I love my own that are just and good, and turn my face away from heathens such as you."

Makar's heart stood still. He felt the disgrace of his own existence. He hung his head, but then suddenly lifted it and was moved to speak again.

Who were these just and good men the Toyon spoke off? Were they those who lived in fine palaces on the earth at the same time as Makar had? If so, Makar knew them. Their eyes were bright because they had not shed as many tears as he had, and their faces were radiant because they were bathed in fragrance, and their clean garments had been made by the hands of others.

Makar's head drooped but then he very quickly raised it again.

Did the Toyon not see that he, too, had been born like the others—with bright, open eyes, in which heaven and earth were reflected, and with a pure heart which was ready to hearken to all that was beautiful in the world. And if he longed now to hide his miserable and shameful self underground, it was no fault of his, nor did he know whose fault it was. The one thing he knew was that there was no patience left in his heart.

VII

Had Makar seen the effect his speech had produced on the old Toyon, had he seen that every word he said fell on the golden scale like a weight of lead, he would have restrained the anger of his heart. But he could see nothing of this, for his heart welled with a blind despair.

He looked back on his past life, which had been so wretched. How had he been able to bear that terrible burden? He had borne it because through the darkness flickered a tiny star of hope. Once when he was alive he thought that perhaps a better lot might still be in store for him. But now that he had advanced toward the end, hope, too, was dead.

Darkness now settled upon his soul, and a fury raged in it, like a storm raging in the steppe in the dead of night. He forgot where he was, before whom he stood—forgot everything save the rage in him …

But the old Toyon said to him:

"Wait, poor man! You are not on earth … There is justice for you here."

And Makar was startled out of his despair. He realized that he was being pitied and his heart softened; his miserable life looming before his gaze, from the first to the last day, he was overcome by pity for himself. He burst into tears.

The old Toyon wept, too, and so did Father Ivan. Tears flowed from the eyes of the young serving men, and they dried them with their white flowing sleeves.

The scales started to swing, with the wooden scale now rising higher and higher!

1883

A WOMAN'S KINGDOM

Anton Chekhov

I

Christmas Eve

Here was a thick roll of notes. It came from the bailiff at the forest villa; he wrote that he was sending fifteen hundred rubles, which he had been awarded as damages, having won an appeal. Anna Akimovna disliked and feared such words as "awarded damages" and "won the suit." She knew that it was impossible to do without the law, but for some reason, whenever Nazaritch, the manager of the factory, or the bailiff of her villa in the country, both of whom frequently went to court, used to win lawsuits of some sort for her benefit, she always felt uneasy and, as it were, ashamed. On this occasion, too, she felt uneasy and awkward, and wanted to put that fifteen hundred rubles farther away that it might be out of her sight.

She thought with vexation that other girls of her age—she was in her twenty-sixth year—were now busy looking after their households, were weary and would sleep sound, and would wake up tomorrow morning in holiday mood; many of them had long been married and had children. Only she, for some reason, was compelled to sit like an old woman over these letters, to make notes upon them, to write answers, then to do nothing the whole evening till midnight, but wait till she was sleepy; and tomorrow they would all day long be coming with Christmas greetings and asking for favors; and the day after tomorrow there would certainly be some scandal at the factory—someone would be beaten or would die of drinking too much vodka, and she would be fretted by pangs of conscience; and after the holidays Nazaritch would turn out some twenty of the workers for absence from work, and all of the twenty would hang about at the front door, without their caps on, and she would be ashamed to go out to them, and they would be driven away like dogs. And all her acquaintances would say behind her back, and write to her in anonymous letters, that she was a millionaire and exploiter—that she was devouring other men's lives and sucking the blood of the workers.

Here there lay a heap of letters read through and laid aside already. They were all begging letters. They were from people who were hungry, drunken, dragged down by large families, sick, degraded, despised … Anna Akimovna had already noted on each letter, three rubles to be paid to one, five to another. These letters would go the same day to the office, and next the distribution of assistance would take place, or, as the clerks used to say, the beasts would be fed.

They would distribute also in small sums four hundred and seventy rubles—the interest on a sum bequeathed by the late Akim Ivanovitch for the relief of the poor and needy. There would be a hideous crush. From the gates to the doors of the office there would stretch a long file of strange people with brutal faces, in rags, numb with cold, hungry, and already drunk, in husky voices calling down blessings upon Anna Akimovna, their benefactress, and her parents. Those at the back would press upon those in front, and those in front would abuse them with bad language. The clerk would get tired of the noise, the swearing, and the singsong whining and blessing, would fly out and give someone a box on the ear to the delight of all. And her own people, the factory hands, who received nothing at Christmas but their wages, and had already spent every kopeck of it, would stand in the middle of the yard, looking on and laughing—some enviously, others ironically.

"Merchants, and still more their wives, are fonder of beggars than they are of their own workers," thought Anna Akimovna. "It's always so."

Her eye fell upon the roll of money. It would be nice to distribute that hateful, useless money among the workers tomorrow, but it did not do to give the workers anything for nothing, or they would demand it again next time. And what would be the good of fifteen hundred rubles when there were eighteen hundred workers in the factory besides their wives and children? Or she might, perhaps, pick out one of the writers of those begging letters—some luckless man who had long ago lost all hope of anything better, and give him the fifteen hundred. The money would come upon the poor creature like a thunderclap, and perhaps for the first time in his life he would feel happy. This idea struck Anna Akimovna as original and amusing, and it fascinated her. She took one letter at random out of the pile and read it. Some petty official called Tchalikov had long been out of a situation, was ill, and living in Gushchin's building; his wife was in consumption, and he had five little girls. Anna Akimovna knew well the four-story house, Gushchin's building, in which Tchalikov lived. Oh, it was a horrid, foul, unhealthy house!

"Well, I will give it to that Tchalikov," she decided. "I won't send it; I had better take it myself to prevent unnecessary talk. Yes," she reflected, as she put the fifteen hundred rubles in her pocket, "and I'll have a look at them, and perhaps I can do something for the little girls."

She felt lighthearted. She rang the bell and ordered the horses to be brought around.

When she got into the sled it was past six o'clock in the evening. The windows in all the blocks of buildings were brightly lighted up, and that made the huge courtyard seem very dark: at the gates, and at the far end of the yard near the warehouses and the workers' barracks, electric lamps were gleaming.

Anna Akimovna disliked and feared those huge dark buildings, warehouses, and barracks where the workers lived. She had only once been in the main building since her father's death. The high ceilings with iron girders, the multitude of huge, rapidly turning wheels, connecting straps and levers, the shrill hissing, the clank of steel, the rattle of the trolleys, the harsh puffing of steam, the faces—pale, crimson, or black with coal dust, the shirts soaked with sweat, the gleam of steel, of copper, and of fire, the smell of oil and coal, and the draft, at times very hot and at times very cold—gave her an impression of hell. It seemed to her as though the wheels, the levers, and the hot hissing cylinders were trying to tear themselves away from their fastenings to crush the men, while the men, not hearing one another, ran about with anxious faces, and busied themselves about the machines, trying to stop their terrible movement. They showed Anna Akimovna something and respectfully explained it to her. She remembered how in the forge a piece of red-hot iron was pulled out of the furnace, and how an old man with a strap around his head, and another, a young man in a blue shirt with a chain on his breast, and an angry face, probably one of the foremen, struck the piece of iron with hammers; and how the golden sparks had been scattered in all directions; and how, a little afterward, they had dragged out a huge piece of sheet iron with a clang. The old man had stood erect and smiled, while the young man had wiped his face with his sleeve and explained something to her. And she remembered, too, how in another department an old man with one eye had been filing a piece of iron, and how the iron filings were scattered about, and how a red-haired man in black spectacles, with holes in his shirt, had been working at a lathe, making something out of a piece of steel: the lathe roared and hissed and squeaked, and Anna Akimovna felt sick at the sound, and it seemed as though they were boring into her ears. She looked, listened, did not understand, smiled graciously, and felt ashamed. To get hundreds of thousands of rubles from a business which one does not understand and cannot like—how strange it is!

And she had not once been in the workers' barracks. There, she was told, it was damp; there were bugs, debauchery, anarchy. It was an astonishing thing: a thousand rubles were spent annually on keeping the barracks in good order, yet, if she were to believe the anonymous letters, the condition of the workers was growing worse and worse every year.

"There was more order in my father's day," thought Anna Akimovna, as she drove out of the yard, "because he had been a workman himself. I know nothing about it and only do silly things."

She felt depressed again, and was no longer glad that she had come, and the thought of the lucky man upon whom fifteen hundred rubles would drop from heaven no longer struck her as original and amusing. To go to some Tchalikov or other, when at home a business worth a million was gradually going to pieces and being ruined, and the workers in the barracks were living worse than convicts, meant doing something silly and cheating her conscience. Along the highway and across the fields near it, workers from the neighboring cotton and paper factories were walking toward the lights of the town. There was the sound of talk and laughter in the frosty air. Anna Akimovna looked at the women and young people, and she suddenly felt a longing for a plain rough life among a crowd. She recalled vividly that faraway time when she used to be called Anyutka, when she was a little girl and used to lie under the same quilt with her mother, while a washerwoman who lodged with them used to wash clothes in the next room, and through the thin walls there came from the neighboring flats sounds of laughter, swearing, children's crying, the accordion, and the whirr of carpenters' lathes and sewing machines. And her father, Akim Ivanovitch, who was clever at almost every craft, would be soldering something near the stove, or drawing or planing, taking no notice whatever of the noise and stuffiness. And she longed to wash, to iron, to run to the shop and the tavern as she used to do every day when she lived with her mother. She ought to have been a work-girl and not the factory owner! Her big house with its chandeliers and pictures; her footman, Mishenka, with his glossy moustache and swallowtail coat; the devout and dignified Varvarushka, and smooth-tongued Agafyushka; and the young people of both sexes who came almost every day to ask her for money, and with whom she always for some reason felt guilty; and the clerks, the doctors, and the ladies who were charitable at her expense, who flattered her and secretly despised her for her humble origin—how wearisome and alien it all was to her!

Here was the railway crossing and the city gate, then came houses alternating with kitchen gardens, and at last the broad street where stood the renowned Gushchin's building. The street, usually quiet, was now on Christmas Eve full of life and movement. The eating-houses and beer shops were noisy. If someone who did not belong to that quarter but lived in the center of the town had driven through the street now, he would have noticed nothing but dirty, drunken, and abusive people. But Anna Akimovna, who had lived in those parts all her life, was constantly recognizing in the crowd her own father or mother or uncle. Her father was a soft fluid character, a little fantastical, frivolous, and irresponsible. He did not care for money, respectability, or power; he used to say that a workingman had no time to keep the holy days and go to church; and if it had not been for his wife, he would probably never have gone to confession, taken the sacrament, or kept the fasts. While her uncle, Ivan Ivanovitch, on the contrary, was like flint; in everything relating to religion, politics, and morality, he was harsh and relentless, and kept a strict watch, not only over himself, but also over all his servants and acquaintances. God forbid that one should go into his room without crossing oneself before the icon! The luxurious mansion in which Anna Akimovna now lived he had always kept locked up, and opened it only on great holidays for important visitors, while he himself lived in the office, in a little room covered with icons. He had leanings toward the Old Believers, and was continually entertaining priests and bishops of the old ritual, though he had been christened, and married, and had buried his wife in accordance with the Orthodox rites. He disliked Akim, his only brother and his heir, for his frivolity, which he called simpleness and folly, and for his indifference to religion. He treated him as an inferior, kept him in the position of a workman, paid him sixteen rubles a month. Akim addressed his brother with formal respect, and on the days of asking forgiveness, he and his wife and daughter bowed down to the ground before him. But three years before his death Ivan Ivanovitch had drawn closer to his brother, forgave his shortcomings, and ordered him to get a governess for Anyutka.

There was a dark, deep, evil-smelling archway under Gushchin's building; there was a sound of men coughing near the walls. Leaving the sled in the street, Anna Akimovna went in at the gate and inquired how to get to No. 46 to see a clerk called Tchalikov. She was directed to the farthest door on the right, on the third floor. And in the courtyard and near the outer door, and even on the stairs, there was still the same loathsome smell as under the archway. In Anna Akimovna's childhood, when her father was a simple workman, she used to live in a building like that, and afterward, when their circumstances were different, she had often visited them in the character of a philanthropist. The narrow stone staircase with its steep dirty steps, with landings at every story; the greasy swinging lanterns; the stench; the troughs, pots, and rags on the landings near the doors—all this had been familiar to her long ago … One door was open, and within could be seen Jewish tailors in caps, sewing. Anna Akimovna met people on the stairs, but it never entered her head that people might be rude to her. She was no more afraid of peasants or workers, drunk or sober, than of her acquaintances of the educated class.

There was no entryway at No. 46, the door opened straight into the kitchen. As a rule the dwellings of workers and mechanics smell of varnish, tar, hides, smoke, according to the occupation of the tenant. The dwellings of persons of noble or official class who have come to poverty may be known by a peculiar rancid, sour smell. This disgusting smell enveloped Anna Akimovna on all sides, and as yet she was only on the threshold. A man in a black coat, no doubt Tchalikov himself, was sitting in a corner at the table with his back to the door, and with him were five little girls. The eldest, a broad-faced thin girl with a comb in her hair, looked about fifteen, while the youngest, a chubby child with hair that stood up like a hedgehog, was not more than three. All the six were eating. Near the stove stood a very thin little woman with a yellow face, far gone in pregnancy. She was wearing a skirt and a white blouse, and had an oven fork in her hand.

"I did not expect you to be so disobedient, Liza," the man was saying reproachfully. "Fie, fie, for shame! Do you want Papa to whip you—eh?"

Seeing an unknown lady in the doorway, the thin woman started, and put down the fork.

"Vassily Nikititch!" she cried, after a pause, in a hollow voice, as though she could not believe her eyes.

The man looked round and jumped up. He was a flat-chested, bony man with narrow shoulders and sunken temples. His eyes were small and hollow with dark rings round them, he had a wide mouth, and a long nose like a bird's beak—a little bit bent to the right. His beard was parted in the middle, his moustache was shaven, and this made him look more like a hired footman than a government clerk.

"Does Mr. Tchalikov live here?" asked Anna Akimovna.

"Yes, madam," Tchalikov answered severely, but immediately recognizing Anna Akimovna, he cried: "Anna Akimovna!" and all at once he gasped and clasped his hands as though in terrible alarm. "Benefactress!"

With a moan he ran to her, grunting inarticulately as though he were paralyzed—there was cabbage on his beard and he smelled of vodka—pressed his forehead to her fur handwarmer, and seemed as though he were in a swoon.

"Your hand, your holy hand!" he brought out breathlessly. "It's a dream, a glorious dream! Children, awaken me!"

He turned towards the table and said in a sobbing voice, shaking his fists:

"Providence has heard us! Our savior, our angel, has come! We are saved! Children, down on your knees! On your knees!"

Madame Tchalikov and the little girls, except the youngest one, began for some reason rapidly clearing the table.

"You wrote that your wife was very ill," said Anna Akimovna, and she felt ashamed and annoyed. "I am not going to give them the fifteen hundred," she thought.

"Here she is, my wife," said Tchalikov in a thin feminine voice, as though his tears had gone to his head. "Here she is, unhappy creature! With one foot in the grave! But we do not complain, madam. Better death than such a life. Better die, unhappy woman!"

"Why is he playing these antics?" thought Anna Akimovna with annoyance. "One can see at once he is used to dealing with merchants."

"Speak to me like a human being," she said. "I don't care for farces."

"Yes, madam. Five bereaved children round their mother's coffin with funeral candles—that's a farce? Eh?" said Tchalikov bitterly, and turned away.

"Hold your tongue," whispered his wife, and she pulled at his sleeve. "The place has not been tidied up, madam," she said, addressing Anna Akimovna. "Please excuse it … You know what it is where there are children. A crowded hearth, but harmony."

"I am not going to give them the fifteen hundred," Anna Akimovna thought again.

And to escape as soon as possible from these people and from the sour smell, she brought out her purse and made up her mind to leave them twenty-five rubles, not more, but she suddenly felt ashamed that she had come so far and disturbed people for so little.

"If you give me paper and ink, I will write at once to a doctor who is a friend of mine to come and see you," she said, flushing red. "He is a very good doctor. And I will leave you some money for medicine."

Madame Tchalikov was hastening to wipe the table.

"It's messy here! What are you doing?" hissed Tchalikov, looking at her wrathfully. "Take her to the lodger's room! I make bold to ask you, madam, to step into the lodger's room," he said, addressing Anna Akimovna. "It's clean there."

"Osip Ilyitch told us not to go into his room!" said one of the little girls, sternly.

But they had already led Anna Akimovna out of the kitchen, through a narrow passage room between two bedsteads: it was evident from the arrangement of the beds that in one two slept lengthwise, and in the other three slept across the bed. In the lodger's room, that came next, it really was clean. A neat-looking bed with a red woolen quilt, a pillow in a white pillowcase, even a slipper for the watch, a table covered with a hempen cloth and on it, an ink-stand of milky-looking glass, pens, paper, photographs in frames—everything as it ought to be. There was another table for rough work, on which lay tidily arranged a watchmaker's tools and watches taken to pieces. On the walls hung hammers, pliers, awls, chisels, nippers, and so on, and there were three hanging clocks which were ticking. One was a big clock with thick weights, such as one sees in eating-houses.

As she sat down to write the letter, Anna Akimovna saw facing her on the table the photographs of her father and of herself. That surprised her.

"Who lives here with you?" she asked.

"Our lodger, madam, Osip Ilyitch Pimenov. He works in your factory."

"Oh, I thought he must be a watchmaker."

"He repairs watches privately, in his leisure hours. He is an amateur."

After a brief silence during which nothing could be heard but the ticking of the clocks and the scratching of the pen on the paper, Tchalikov heaved a sigh and said ironically, with indignation:

"It's a true saying: gentle birth and a grade in the service won't put a coat on your back. A cockade in your cap and a noble title, but nothing to eat. To my thinking, if anyone of humble class helps the poor he is much more of a gentleman than any Tchalikov who has sunk into poverty and vice."

To flatter Anna Akimovna, he uttered a few more disparaging phrases about his gentle birth, and it was evident that he was humbling himself because he considered himself superior to her. Meanwhile she had finished her letter and had sealed it up. The letter would be thrown away and the money would not be spent on medicine—that she knew, but she put twenty-five rubles on the table all the same, and after a moment's thought, added two more red notes. She saw the wasted, yellow hand of Madame Tchalikov, like the claw of a hen, dart out and clutch the money tight.

"You have graciously given this for medicine," said Tchalikov in a quivering voice, "but hold out a helping hand to me also … and the children!" he added with a sob. "My unhappy children! I am not afraid for myself. It is for my daughters I fear! It's the hydra of vice that I fear!"

Trying to open her purse, the catch of which had gone wrong, Anna Akimovna was confused and turned red. She felt ashamed that people should be standing before her, looking at her hands and waiting, and most likely at the bottom of their hearts laughing at her. At that instant someone came into the kitchen and stamped his feet, knocking the snow off.

"The lodger has come in," said Madame Tchalikov.

Anna Akimovna grew even more confused. She did not want anyone from the factory to find her in this ridiculous position. As ill luck would have it, the lodger came in at the very moment when, having broken the catch at last, she was giving Tchalikov some notes, and Tchalikov, grunting as though he were paralyzed, was feeling about with his lips where he could kiss her. In the lodger she recognized the workman who had once clanked the sheet iron before her in the forge, and had explained things to her. Evidently he had come in straight from the factory; his face looked dark and grimy, and on one cheek near his nose was a smudge of soot. His hands were perfectly black, and his unbelted shirt shone with oil and grease. He was a man of thirty, of medium height, with black hair and broad shoulders, and a look of great physical strength. At the first glance Anna Akimovna perceived that he must be a foreman, who must be receiving at least thirty-five rubles a month, and a stern, loud-voiced man who struck the workers in the face. All this was evident from his manner of standing, from the attitude he involuntarily assumed at once on seeing a lady in his room, and most of all from the fact that he did not wear topboots, that he had breast pockets, and a pointed, picturesquely clipped beard. Her father, Akim Ivanovitch, had been the brother of the factory owner, and yet he had been afraid of foremen like this lodger and had tried to win their favor.

"Excuse me for having come in here in your absence," said Anna Akimovna.

The workman looked at her in surprise, smiled in confusion and did not speak.

"You must speak a little louder, madam ..." said Tchalikov softly. "When Mr. Pimenov comes home from the factory in the evenings he is a little hard of hearing."

But Anna Akimovna was by now relieved that there was nothing more for her to do here. She nodded to them and went rapidly out of the room. Pimenov went to see her out.

"Have you been long in our employment?" she asked in a loud voice, without turning to him.

"From nine years old. I entered the factory in your uncle's time."

"That's a long while! My uncle and my father knew all the workers, and I know hardly any of them. I had seen you before, but I did not know your name was Pimenov."

Anna Akimovna felt a desire to justify herself before him, to pretend that she had just given the money not seriously, but as a joke.

"Oh, this poverty," she sighed. "We give charity on holidays and working days, and still there is no sense in it. I believe it is useless to help such people as this Tchalikov."

"Of course it is useless," he agreed. "However much you give him, he will drink it all away. And now the husband and wife will be snatching it from one another and fighting all night," he added with a laugh.

"Yes, one must admit that our philanthropy is useless, boring, and absurd. But still, you must agree, one can't sit with one's hand in one's lap; one must do something. What's to be done with the Tchalikovs, for instance?"

She turned to Pimenov and stopped, expecting an answer from him; he, too, stopped and slowly, without speaking, shrugged his shoulders. Obviously he knew what to do with the Tchalikovs, but the treatment would have been so coarse and inhuman that he did not venture to put it into words. And the Tchalikovs were to him so utterly uninteresting and worthless, that a moment later he had forgotten them. Looking into Anna Akimovna's eyes, he smiled with pleasure, and his face wore an expression as though he were dreaming about something very pleasant. Only, now standing close to him, Anna Akimovna saw from his face, and especially from his eyes, how exhausted and sleepy he was.

"Here, I ought to give him the fifteen hundred rubles!" she thought, but for some reason this idea seemed to her incongruous and insulting to Pimenov.

"I am sure you are aching all over after your work, and you come to the door with me," she said as they went down the stairs. "Go home."

But he did not catch her words. When they came out into the street, he ran on ahead, unfastened the cover of the sled, and helping Anna Akimovna in, said:

"I wish you a happy Christmas!"

II

Christmas Morning

"They have ceased ringing ever so long! It's dreadful, you won't be there before the service is over! Get up!"

"Two horses are racing, racing ..." said Anna Akimovna, and she woke up; before her, candle in hand, stood her maid, red-haired Masha. "Well, what is it?"

"Service is over already," said Masha with despair. "I have called you three times! Sleep till evening for me, but you told me yourself to call you!"

Anna Akimovna raised herself on her elbow and glanced toward the window. It was still quite dark outside, and only the lower edge of the window frame was white with snow. She could hear a low, mellow chime of bells; it was not the parish church, but somewhere farther away. The clock on the little table showed three minutes past six.

"Very well, Masha ... In three minutes ..." said Anna Akimovna in an imploring voice, and she snuggled under the bedclothes.

She imagined the snow at the front door, the sled, the dark sky, the crowd in the church, and the smell of juniper, and she felt dread at the thought, but all the same, she made up her mind that she would get up at once and go to early service. And while she was warm in bed and struggling with sleep—

which seems, as though to spite one, particularly sweet when one ought to get up—and while she had visions of an immense garden on a mountain and then Gushchin's building, she was worried all the time by the thought that she ought to get up that very minute and go to church.

But when she got up it was quite light, and it turned out to be half past nine. There had been a heavy fall of snow in the night; the trees were clothed in white, and the air was particularly light, transparent, and tender, so that when Anna Akimovna looked out of the window her first impulse was to draw a deep, deep breath. And when she had washed, a relic of faraway childish feelings—joy that today was Christmas—suddenly stirred within her. After that she felt lighthearted, free, and pure in soul, as though her soul, too, had been washed or plunged in the white snow. Masha came in, dressed up and tightly laced, and wished her a happy Christmas; then she spent a long time combing her mistress's hair and helping her to dress. The fragrance and feeling of the new, gorgeoús, splendid dress, its faint rustle, and the smell of fresh scent, excited Anna Akimovna.

"Well, it's Christmas," she said gaily to Masha. "Now we will try our fortunes."

"Last year, I was to marry an old man. It turned up three times the same."

"Well, God is merciful."

"Well, Anna Akimovna, what I think is, rather than neither one thing nor the other, I'd marry an old man," said Masha mournfully, and she heaved a sigh. "I am turned twenty; it's no joke."

Everyone in the house knew that red-haired Masha was in love with Mishenka, the footman, and this genuine, passionate, hopeless love had already lasted three years.

"Come, don't talk nonsense," Anna Akimovna consoled her. "I am going on thirty, but I am still meaning to marry a young man."

While his mistress was dressing, Mishenka, in a new swallowtail and polished boots, walked about the hall and drawing room and waited for her to come out, to wish her a happy Christmas. He had a peculiar walk, stepping softly and delicately. Looking at his feet, his hands, and the bend of his head, it might be imagined that he was not simply walking, but learning to dance the first figure of a quadrille. In spite of his fine velvety moustache and handsome, rather flashy appearance, he was steady, prudent, and devout as an old man. He said his prayers, bowing down to the ground, and liked burning incense in his room. He respected people of wealth and rank and had a reverence for them; he despised poor people, and all who came to ask favors of any kind, with all the strength of his cleanly flunky soul. Under his starched shirt he wore a flannel, winter and summer alike, being very careful of his health. His ears were plugged with cotton wool.

When Anna Akimovna crossed the hall with Masha, he bent his head downward a little and said in his agreeable, honeyed voice:

"I have the honor to congratulate you, Anna Akimovna, on the most solemn feast of the birth of our Lord."

Anna Akimovna gave him five rubles, while poor Masha was numb with ecstasy. His holiday getup, his attitude, his voice, and what he said, impressed her by their beauty and elegance; as she followed her mistress she could think of nothing, could see nothing, she could only smile, first blissfully and then bitterly.

The upper story of the house was called the pure or noble rooms, while the rooms on the lower story, where business was conducted and where Aunt Tatyana Ivanovna kept house, were called the old people's or simply the women's rooms. In the upper part the gentry and educated visitors were entertained; in the lower story, simpler folk and the aunt's personal friends. Pretty, plump, and healthy, still young and fresh, and feeling she had on a magnificent dress which seemed to her to diffuse a sort of radiance all about her, Anna Akimovna went down to the lower story. Here she was met with reproaches for forgetting God now that she was so highly educated, for sleeping too late for the service, and for not coming downstairs to break the fast, and they all clasped their hands and exclaimed with perfect sincerity that she was lovely, wonderful; and she believed it, laughed, kissed them, gave one a ruble, another three or five according to their position. She liked being downstairs. Wherever one looked there were shrines, icons, little lamps, portraits of ecclesiastical personages—the place smelled of monks; there was a rattle of knives in the kitchen, and already a smell of something savory, exceedingly appetizing, was pervading all the rooms. The yellow-painted floors shone, and from the doors narrow rugs with bright blue stripes ran like little paths to the icon corner, and the sunshine was simply pouring in at the windows.

In the dining room some old women, strangers, were sitting. In Varvarushka's room, too, there were old women, and with them a deaf and dumb girl, who seemed abashed about something and kept saying, "Bly, bly!" Two skinny-looking little girls who had been brought out of the orphanage for Christmas came up to kiss Anna Akimovna's hand, and stood before her transfixed with admiration of her splendid dress. She noticed that one of the girls squinted, and in the midst of her lighthearted holiday mood she felt a sick pang at her heart at the thought that young men would despise the girl, and that she would never marry. In the cook Agafya's room, five huge peasants in new shirts were sitting around the samovar. These were not workers from the factory, but relations of the cook. Seeing Anna Akimovna, all the peasants jumped up from their seats, and out of regard for decorum, ceased munching, though their mouths were full. The cook, Stepan, in a white cap, with a knife in his hand, came into the room and gave her his greetings; porters in high felt boots came in, and they, too, offered their greetings. The water carrier peeped in with icicles on his beard, but did not venture to enter.

Anna Akimovna walked through the rooms followed by her retinue—the aunt, Varvarushka, Nikandrovna, the sewing-maid, Marfa Petrovna, and the downstairs Masha. Varvarushka—a tall, thin, slender woman, taller than anyone in the house, dressed all in black, smelling of cypress and coffee—crossed herself in each room before the icon, bowing down from the waist. And whenever one looked at her one was reminded that she had already prepared her own funeral shroud and that lottery tickets were hidden away by her in the same box.

"Anyutinka, be merciful at Christmas," she said, opening the door into the kitchen. "Forgive him, bless the man! Have done with it!"

The coachman, Pantelei, who had been dismissed for drunkenness in November, was on his knees in the middle of the kitchen. He was a good-natured man, but he used to be unruly when he was drunk, and could not go to sleep, but persisted in wandering about the buildings and shouting in a threatening voice, "I know all about it!" Now from his beefy and bloated face and from his bloodshot eyes it could be seen that he had been drinking continually from November till Christmas.

"Forgive me, Anna Akimovna," he brought out in a hoarse voice, striking his forehead on the floor and showing his bull-like neck.

"It was Auntie who dismissed you, ask her."

"What about Auntie?" said her aunt, walking into the kitchen, breathing heavily. She was very stout, and on her bosom one might have stood a tray of teacups and a samovar. "What about Auntie now? You are mistress here, give your own orders; though these rascals might all be dead for all I care. Come, get up, you hog!" she shouted at Pantelei, losing patience. "Get out of my sight! It's the last time I forgive you, but if you transgress again—don't ask for mercy!"

Then they went into the dining room for coffee. But they had hardly sat down when the downstairs Masha rushed headlong in, saying with horror, "The singers!" And ran back again. They heard someone blowing his nose, a low bass cough, and footsteps that sounded like horses' iron-shod hoofs tramping about the entry near the hall. For half a minute all was hushed ... The singers burst out so suddenly and loudly that everyone started. While they were singing, the priest from the almshouses arrived with the deacon and the sexton. Putting on the stole, the priest slowly said that when they were ringing for matins it was snowing and not cold, but that the frost was sharper toward morning, God bless it, and now there must be twenty degrees of frost.

"Many people maintain, though, that winter is healthier than summer," said the deacon, then immediately assumed an austere expression and chanted after the priest. "Thy Birth, O Christ, Our Lord ..."

Soon the priest from the workers' hospital came with the deacon, then the Sisters from the hospital, children from the orphanage, and then singing could be heard almost uninterruptedly. They sang, had lunch, and went away.

About twenty men from the factory came to offer their Christmas greetings. They were only the foremen, mechanics, and their assistants, the pattern-makers, the accountant, and so on—all of good appearance, in new black coats. They were all first-rate men, chosen men, as it were. Each one knew his value—that is, knew that if he lost his berth today, people would be glad to take him on at another factory. Evidently they liked Auntie, as they behaved freely in her presence and even smoked, and when they had all trooped in to have something to eat, the accountant put his arm round her immense waist. They were free and easy, perhaps, partly also because Varvarushka, who under the old masters had wielded great power and had kept watch over the morals of the clerks, had now no authority whatever in the house; and perhaps because many of them still remembered the time when Auntie Tatyana Ivanovna, whose brothers kept a strict hand over her, had been dressed like a simple peasant woman like Agafya, and when Anna Akimovna used to run about the yard near the factory buildings and everyone used to call her Anyutya.

The foremen ate, talked, and kept looking with amazement at Anna Akimovna, how she had grown up and how pretty she had become! But this elegant girl, educated by governesses and teachers, was a stranger to them; they could not understand her, and they instinctively kept closer to "Auntie," who called them by their names, continually pressed them to eat and drink, and, clinking glasses with them, had already drunk two glasses of rowanberry wine with them. Anna Akimovna was always afraid of their thinking her proud, an upstart, or a crow in peacock's feathers, and now while the foremen were crowding around the food, she did not leave the dining room, but took part in the conversation. She asked Pimenov, her acquaintance of the previous day:

"Why have you so many clocks in your room?"

"I mend clocks," he answered. "I take the work up between times, on holidays, or when I can't sleep."

"So if my watch goes wrong I can bring it to you to be repaired?" Anna Akimovna asked, laughing.

"To be sure, I will do it with pleasure," said Pimenov, and there was an expression of tender devotion in his face, when, not knowing why herself, she unfastened her magnificent watch from its chain and handed it to him. He looked at it in silence and gave it back. "To be sure, I will do it with pleasure," he repeated. "I don't mend watches now. My eyes are weak, and the doctors have forbidden me to do fine work. But for you I can make an exception."

"Doctors talk nonsense," said the accountant. They all laughed. "Don't you believe them," he went on, flattered by the laughing, "last year a tooth flew out of a cylinder and hit old Kalmykov such a crack on the head that you could see his brains, and the doctor said he would die. But he is alive and working to this day, only he has taken to stammering since that mishap."

"Doctors do talk nonsense, they do, but not so much," sighed Auntie. "Piotr Andreyitch, poor dear, lost his sight. Just like you, he used to work day in day out at the factory near the hot furnace, and he went blind. The eyes don't like heat. But what are we talking about?" she said, rousing herself. "Come and have a drink. My best wishes for Christmas, my dears. I never drink with anyone else, but I drink with you, sinful woman as I am. God bless!"

Anna Akimovna fancied that after yesterday Pimenov despised her as a philanthropist, but was fascinated by her as a woman. She looked at him and thought that he behaved very charmingly and was nicely dressed. It is true that the sleeves of his coat were not quite long enough, and the coat itself seemed short-waisted, and his trousers were not wide and fashionable, but his tie was tied jauntily and with taste and was not as gaudy as the others'. And he seemed to be a good-natured man, for he ate submissively whatever Auntie put on his plate. She remembered how black he had been the day before, and how sleepy, and the thought of it for some reason touched her.

When the men were preparing to go, Anna Akimovna put out her hand to Pimenov. She wanted to ask him to come in sometimes to see her, without ceremony, but she did not know how to—her tongue would not obey her—and that they might not think she was attracted to Pimenov, she shook hands with his companions, too.

Then the boys from the school of which she was a patroness came. They all had their heads closely cropped and wore gray blouses of the same pattern. The teacher—a tall, beardless young man with patches of red on his face—was visibly agitated as he formed the boys into rows. The boys sang in tune, but with harsh, disagreeable voices. The manager of the factory, Nazaritch, a bald, sharp-eyed Old Believer, could never get on with the teachers, but the one who was now anxiously waving his hands he despised and hated, though he could not have said why. He behaved rudely and condescendingly to the young man, kept back his salary, meddled with the teaching, and had finally tried to dislodge him by appointing, a fortnight before Christmas, as porter to the school a drunken peasant, a distant relation of his wife's, who disobeyed the teacher and said rude things to him before the boys.

Anna Akimovna was aware of all this, but she could be of no help, for she was afraid of Nazaritch herself. Now she wanted at least to be very nice to the schoolmaster, to tell him she was very much pleased with him, but when after the singing he began apologizing for something in great confusion, and Auntie began to address him familiarly as she drew him without ceremony to the table, she felt, for some reason, bored and awkward. Giving orders that the children should be given sweets, she went upstairs.

"In reality there is something cruel in these Christmas customs," she said a little while afterward, as it were to herself, looking out of the window at the boys, who were flocking from the house to the gates and shivering with cold, putting their coats on as they ran. "At Christmas one wants to rest, to sit at home with one's own people, and the poor boys, the teacher, and the clerks and foremen, are obliged for some reason to go through the frost, then to offer their greetings, show their respect, be put to confusion …"

Mishenka, who was standing at the door of the drawing room and overheard this, said:

"It has not come from us, and it will not end with us. Of course, I am not an educated man, Anna Akimovna, but I do understand that the poor must always respect the rich. It is well said, 'God marks the rogue.' In prisons, night refuges, and pothouses you never see any but the poor, while decent people, you may notice, are always rich. It has been said of the rich, 'Deep calls to deep.'"

"You always express yourself so tediously and incomprehensibly," said Anna Akimovna, and she walked to the other end of the big drawing room.

It was only just past eleven. The stillness of the big room, broken only by the singing that floated up from below, made her yawn. The bronzes, the albums, and the pictures on the walls, representing a ship at sea, cows in a meadow, and views of the Rhine, were so absolutely stale that her eyes simply glided over them without observing them. The holiday mood was already growing tedious. As before, Anna Akimovna felt that she was beautiful, good-natured, and wonderful, but now it seemed to her that that was of no use to anyone; it seemed to her that she did not know for whom and for what she had put on this expensive dress, too, and, as always happened on all holidays, she began to be fretted by loneliness and the persistent thought that her beauty, her health, and her wealth, were a mere cheat, since she was not wanted, was of no use to anyone, and nobody loved her. She walked through all the rooms, humming and looking out of the window. Stopping in the drawing room, she could not resist beginning to talk to Mishenka.

"I don't know what you think of yourself, Misha," she said, and heaved a sigh. "Really, God might punish you for it."

"What do you mean?"

"You know what I mean. Excuse my meddling in your affairs. But it seems you are spoiling your own life out of obstinacy. You'll admit that it is high time you got married, and she is an excellent and deserving girl. You will never find anyone better. She's a beauty, clever, gentle, and devoted … And her appearance! … If she belonged to our circle or a higher one, people would be falling in love with her for her red hair alone. See how beautifully her hair goes with her complexion. Oh, goodness! You don't understand anything, and don't know what you want," Anna Akimovna said bitterly, and tears came into her eyes. "Poor girl, I am so sorry for her! I know you want a wife with money, but I have told you already I will give Masha a dowry."

Mishenka could not picture his future spouse in his imagination except as a tall, plump, substantial, pious woman, stepping like a peacock, and, for some reason, with a long shawl over her shoulders; while Masha was thin, slender, tightly laced, and walked with little steps, and, worst of all, she was too fascinating and at times extremely attractive to Mishenka, and that, in his opinion, was incongruous with matrimony and in keeping only with loose behavior. When Anna Akimovna had promised to give Masha a dowry, he had hesitated for a time, but once, a poor student in a brown overcoat over his uniform, coming with a letter for Anna Akimovna, was fascinated by Masha, and could not resist embracing her near the hat stand, and she had uttered a faint shriek. Mishenka, standing on the stairs above, had seen this, and from that time had begun to cherish a feeling of disgust for Masha. A poor student! Who knows, if she had been embraced by a rich student or an officer the consequences might have been different.

"Why don't you wish it?" Anna Akimovna asked. "What more do you want?"

Mishenka was silent and looked at the armchair fixedly, and raised his eyebrows.

"Do you love someone else?"

Silence. The red-haired Masha came in with letters and visiting cards on a tray. Guessing that they were talking about her, she blushed to tears.

"The postmen have come," she muttered. "And there is a clerk called Tchalikov waiting below. He says you told him to come today for something."

"What insolence!" said Anna Akimovna, moved to anger. "I gave him no orders. Tell him to take himself off. Say I am not at home!"

A ring was heard. It was the priests from her parish. They were always shown into the aristocratic part of the house—that is, upstairs. After the priests, Nazaritch, the manager of the factory, came to pay his visit, and then the factory doctor; then Mishenka announced the inspector of the elementary schools. Visitors kept arriving.

When there was a moment free, Anna Akimovna sat down in a deep armchair in the drawing room, and shutting her eyes, thought that her loneliness was quite natural because she had not married and never would marry … But that was not her fault. Fate itself had flung her out of the simple working-class surroundings in which, if she could trust her memory, she had felt so snug and at home, into these immense rooms, where she could never think what to do with herself, and could not understand why so many people kept passing before her eyes. What was happening now seemed to her trivial, useless, since it did not and could not give her happiness for one minute.

"If I could fall in love," she thought, stretching. The very thought of this sent a rush of warmth to her heart. "And if I could escape from the factory …" she mused, imagining how the weight of those factory buildings, barracks, and schools would roll off her conscience, roll off her mind … Then she remembered her father, and thought if he had lived longer he would certainly have married her to a workingman—to Pimenov, for instance. He would have told her to marry, and that would have been all about it. And it would have been a good thing; then the factory would have passed into capable hands.

She pictured his curly head, his bold profile, his delicate, ironical lips and the strength, the tremendous strength, in his shoulders, in his arms, in his chest, and the tenderness with which he had looked at her watch that day.

"Well," she said, "it would have been all right. I would have married him."

"Anna Akimovna," said Mishenka, coming noiselessly into the drawing room.

"How you frightened me!" she said, trembling all over. "What do you want?"

"Anna Akimovna," he said, laying his hand on his heart and raising his eyebrows, "you are my mistress and my benefactress, and no one but you can tell me what I ought to do about marriage, for you are as good as a mother to me … But kindly forbid them to laugh and jeer at me downstairs. They won't let me pass without it."

"How do they jeer at you?"

"They call me Mashenka's Mishenka."

"Fooh, what nonsense!" cried Anna Akimovna indignantly. "How stupid you all are! And how stupid you are, Misha! How sick I am of you! I can't bear the sight of you."

III

Dinner

Just as the year before, the last to pay her a visit were Krylin, an actual civil councilor, and Lysevitch, a well-known barrister. It was already dark when they arrived. Krylin, a man of sixty, with a wide mouth and gray whiskers close to his ears, with a face like a lynx, was wearing a uniform with a ribbon of the Order of St. Anna, and white trousers. He held Anna Akimovna's hand in both of his for a long while, looked intently in her face, moved his lips, and at last said, drawling upon one note:

"I used to respect your uncle … and your father, and enjoyed the privilege of their friendship. Now I feel it an agreeable duty, as you see, to present my Christmas wishes to their honored heiress in spite of my infirmities and the distance I have to come … And I am very glad to see you in good health."

The lawyer Lysevitch, a tall, handsome, fair man, with a slight sprinkling of gray on his temples and beard, was distinguished by exceptionally elegant manners; he walked with a swaying step, bowed as it were reluctantly, and shrugged his shoulders as he talked, and all this with an indolent grace, like a spoiled horse fresh from the stable. He was well fed, extremely healthy, and very well-off; on one occasion he had won forty thousand rubles, but concealed the fact from his friends. He was fond of good fare, especially cheese, truffles, and grated radish with hemp oil; while in Paris he had eaten, so he said, fried, unwashed intestine. He spoke smoothly, fluently, without hesitation, and only occasionally, for the sake of effect, permitted himself to hesitate and snap his fingers as if picking up a word. He had long ceased to believe in anything he had to say in the law courts, or perhaps he did believe in it, but attached no kind of significance to it—it had all so long been familiar, stale, ordinary … He believed in nothing but what was original and unusual. A copybook moral in an original form would move him to tears. Both his notebooks were filled with extraordinary expressions which he had read in various authors, and when he needed to look up any expression, he would search nervously in both books, and usually failed to find it. Anna Akimovna's father had in a good-humored moment ostentatiously appointed him legal adviser in matters concerning the factory, and had assigned him a salary of twelve thousand rubles. The legal business of the factory had been confined to two or three trivial actions for recovering debts, which Lysevitch handed to his assistants.

Anna Akimovna knew that he had nothing to do at the factory, but she could not dismiss him: she had not the moral courage and besides, she was used to him. He used to call himself her legal adviser, and his salary, which he invariably sent for on the first of the month punctually, he used to call "stern prose." Anna Akimovna knew that when, after her father's death, the timber of her forest was sold for railway sleepers, Lysevitch had made more than fifteen thousand out of the transaction, and had shared it with Nazaritch. When first she found out they had cheated her she had wept bitterly, but afterward she had grown used to it.

Wishing her a happy Christmas, and kissing both her hands, he looked her up and down, and frowned.

"You mustn't," he said with genuine disappointment. "I have told you, my dear, you mustn't!"

"What do you mean, Viktor Nikolaitch?"

"I have told you you mustn't get fat. All your family have an unfortunate tendency to grow fat. You mustn't," he repeated in an imploring voice, and kissed her hand. "You are so handsome! You are so splendid! Here, Your Excellency, let me introduce the one woman in the world whom I have ever seriously loved."

"There is nothing surprising in that. To know Anna Akimovna at your age and not to be in love with her, that would be impossible."

"I adore her," the lawyer continued with perfect sincerity, but with his usual indolent grace. "I love her, but not because I am a man and she is a woman. When I am with her I always feel as though she belongs to some third sex, and I to a fourth, and we float away together into the domain of the subtlest shades, and there we blend into the spectrum. Leconte de Lisle defines such relations better than anyone. He has a superb passage, a marvelous passage …"

Lysevitch rummaged in one notebook, then in the other, and, not finding the quotation, subsided. They began talking of the weather, of the opera, of the arrival, expected shortly, of Duse. Anna Akimovna remembered that the year before Lysevitch and, she seemed to recall, Krylin, too, had dined with her, and now when they were getting ready to go away, she began with perfect sincerity pointing out to them in an imploring voice that as they had no more visits to pay, they ought to remain to dinner with her. After some hesitation the visitors agreed.

In addition to the family dinner, consisting of cabbage soup, suckling pig, goose with apples, and so on, a so-called "French" or "chef's" dinner used to be prepared in the kitchen on great holidays, in case any visitor in the upper story wanted a meal. When they heard the clatter of crockery in the dining room, Lysevitch began to betray a noticeable excitement. He rubbed his hands, shrugged his shoulders, screwed up his eyes, and described with feeling what dinners her father and uncle used to give at one time, and what a marvelous matelote of burbot the cook here could make: it was not a matelote, but a veritable revelation! He was already gloating over the dinner, already eating it in imagination and enjoying it. When Anna Akimovna took his arm and led him to the dining room, he tossed off a glass of vodka and put a piece of salmon in his mouth, then he positively purred with pleasure. He munched loudly, disgustingly, emitting sounds from his nose, while his eyes grew oily and rapacious.

The hors d'oeuvres were superb: among other things, there were fresh white mushrooms stewed in cream, and sauce Provençale made of fried oysters and crayfish, strongly flavored with some bitter pickles. The dinner, consisting of elaborate holiday dishes, was excellent, and so were the wines. Mishenka waited at table with enthusiasm. When he laid some new dish on the table and lifted the shining cover, or poured out the wine, he did it with the solemnity of a professor of black magic, and, looking at his face and his movements suggesting the first figure of a quadrille, the lawyer thought several times, "What a fool!"

After the third course Lysevitch said, turning to Anna Akimovna:

"The *fin de siècle* woman—I mean when she is young, and of course wealthy—must be independent, clever, elegant, intellectual, bold, and a little depraved. Depraved within limits, a little; for excess, you know, is wearisome. You ought not to vegetate, my dear; you ought not to live like everyone else, but to get the full savor of life, and a slight flavor of depravity is the sauce of life. Revel among flowers of intoxicating fragrance, breathe the perfume of musk, eat hashish, and best of all, love, love, love … To begin with, in your place I would set up seven lovers—one for each day of the week—and one I would call Monday, one Tuesday, the third Wednesday, and so on, so that each might know his day."

This conversation troubled Anna Akimovna; she ate nothing and drank only a glass of wine.

"Let me speak at last," she said. "For myself personally, I can't conceive of love without family life. I am lonely, lonely as the moon in the sky, and a waning moon, too, and whatever you may say, I am convinced, I feel that this waning can only be restored by love in its ordinary sense. It seems to me that such love would define my duties, my work, make clear my conception of life. I want from love peace in soul, tranquility; I want the very opposite of musk, and spiritualism, and fin de siècle … in short"—she grew embarrassed—"a husband and children."

"You want to be married? Well, you can do that, too," Lysevitch assented. "You ought to have all experiences: marriage, and jealousy, and the sweetness of the first infidelity, and even children … But make haste and live—make haste, my dear: time is passing. It won't wait."

"Yes, I'll go and get married!" she said, looking angrily at his well-fed, satisfied face. "I will marry in the simplest, most ordinary way and be radiant with happiness. And, would you believe it, I will marry some plain workingman, some mechanic or draughtsman."

"There is no harm in that either. The Duchess Josiana loved Gwynplaine, and that was permissible for her because she was a grand duchess. Everything is permissible for you, too, because you are an exceptional woman: if, my dear, you want to love a black man or an Arab, don't scruple; send for a black man. Don't deny yourself anything. You ought to be as bold as your desires. Don't fall short of them."

"Can it be so hard to understand me?" Anna Akimovna asked with amazement, and her eyes were bright with tears. "Understand, I have an immense business on my hands—two thousand workers, for whom I must answer before God. The men who work for me grow blind and deaf. I am afraid to go on like this. I am afraid! I am wretched, and you have the cruelty to talk to me of black men and … and you smile!" Anna Akimovna brought her fist down on the table. "To go on living the life I am living now, or to marry someone as idle and incompetent as myself, would be a crime. I can't go on living like this," she said hotly, "I cannot!"

"How handsome she is!" said Lysevitch, fascinated by her. "My God, how handsome! But why are you angry, my dear? Perhaps I am wrong, but surely you don't imagine that if, for the sake of ideas for which I have the deepest respect, you renounce the joys of life and lead a dreary existence, your workers will be any the better for it? Not a scrap! No, frivolity, frivolity!" he said decisively. "It's essential for you, it's your duty to be frivolous and depraved! Ponder that, my dear, ponder it."

Anna Akimovna was glad she had spoken out, and her spirits rose. She was pleased she had spoken so well, and that her ideas were so fine and just, and she was already convinced that if Pimenov, for instance, loved her, she would marry him with pleasure.

Mishenka began to pour out champagne.

"You make me angry, Viktor Nikolaitch," she said, clinking glasses with the lawyer. "It seems to me you give advice and know nothing of life yourself. According to you, if a man be a mechanic or a draughtsman, he is bound to be a peasant and an ignoramus! But they are the cleverest people! Extraordinary people!"

"Your uncle and father … I knew them and respected them"—said Krylin, pausing for emphasis; he had been sitting upright as a post, eating steadily the whole time—"they were people of considerable intelligence and … of lofty spiritual qualities."

"Oh, to be sure, we know all about their qualities," the lawyer muttered, and asked permission to smoke.

When dinner was over Krylin was led away for a nap. Lysevitch finished his cigar, and, staggering from repletion, followed Anna Akimovna into her study. Cozy corners with photographs and fans on the walls, and the inevitable pink or pale blue lanterns in the middle of the ceiling, he did not like, as the expression of an insipid and unoriginal character. Besides, the memory of certain of his love affairs of which he was now ashamed was associated with such lanterns. Anna Akimovna's study with its bare walls and tasteless furniture pleased him exceedingly. It was snug and comfortable for him to sit on a Turkish divan and look at Anna Akimovna, who usually sat on the rug before the fire, clasping her knees and looking into the fire and thinking of something, and at such moments it seemed to him that her peasant Old Believer blood was stirring within her.

Every time after dinner when coffee and liqueurs were served, he grew livelier and began telling her various bits of literary gossip. He spoke with eloquence and inspiration, and was carried away by his own stories; she listened to him and thought every time that for such enjoyment it was worth paying not only twelve thousand, but three times that sum, and forgave him everything she disliked in him. He sometimes told her the story of some tale or novel he had been reading, and then two or three hours passed unnoticed like a minute. Now he began rather dolefully in a failing voice with his eyes shut.

"It's ages, my dear, since I have read anything," he said when she asked him to tell her something. "Though I do sometimes read Jules Verne."

"I was expecting you to tell me something new."

"Hmm, new," Lysevitch muttered sleepily, and he settled himself farther back in the corner of the sofa. "None of the new literature, my dear, is any use for you or me. Of course, it is bound to be such as it is, and to refuse to recognize it is to refuse to recognize—would mean refusing to recognize the natural order of things, and I do recognize it, but ..." Lysevitch seemed to have fallen asleep. But a minute later his voice was heard again:

"All the new literature moans and howls like the autumn wind in the chimney. 'Ah, unhappy wretch! Ah, your life may be likened to a prison! Ah, how damp and dark it is in your prison! Ah, you will certainly come to ruin, and there is no chance of escape for you!' That's very fine, but I should prefer a literature that would tell us how to escape from prison. Of all contemporary writers, however, I prefer Maupassant." Lysevitch opened his eyes. "A fine writer, a perfect writer!" Lysevitch shifted in his seat. "A wonderful artist! A terrible, prodigious, supernatural artist!" Lysevitch got up from the sofa and raised his right arm. "Maupassant!" he said rapturously. "My dear, read Maupassant! One page of his gives you more than all the riches of the earth! Every line is a new horizon. The softest, tenderest impulses of the soul alternate with violent, tempestuous sensations. Your soul, as though under the weight of forty thousand atmospheres, is transformed into the most insignificant little bit of some great thing of an undefined rosy hue which I fancy, if one could put it on one's tongue, would yield a pungent, voluptuous taste. What a fury of transitions, of motives, of melodies! You rest peacefully on the lilies and the roses, and suddenly a thought—a terrible, splendid, irresistible thought—swoops down upon you like a locomotive, and bathes you in hot steam and deafens you with its whistle. Read Maupassant, dear girl; I insist on it."

Lysevitch waved his arms and paced from corner to corner in violent excitement.

"Yes, it is inconceivable," he pronounced, as though in despair, "his last thing overwhelmed me, intoxicated me! But I am afraid you will not care for it. To be carried away by it you must savor it, slowly suck the juice from each line, drink it in … You must drink it in!"

After a long introduction, containing many words such as demonic sensuality, a network of the most delicate nerves, simoom, crystal, and so on, he began at last telling the story of the novel. He did not tell the story so whimsically, but told it in minute detail, quoting from memory whole descriptions and conversations. The characters of the novel fascinated him, and to describe them he threw himself into attitudes, changed the expression of his face and voice like a real actor. He laughed with delight at one moment in a deep bass, and at another, on a high shrill note, clasped his hands and clutched at his head with an expression that suggested that it was just going to burst. Anna Akimovna listened enthralled, though she had already read the novel, and it seemed to her ever so much finer and more subtle in the lawyer's version than in the book itself. He drew her attention to various subtleties, and emphasized the felicitous expressions and the profound thoughts, but she saw in it only life, life, life and herself, as though she had been a character in the novel. Her spirits rose, and she, too, laughing and clasping her hands, thought that she could not go on living such a life, that there was no need to have a wretched life when one might have a splendid one. She remembered her words and thoughts at dinner, and was proud of them; and when Pimenov suddenly rose up in her imagination, she felt happy and longed for him to love her.

When he had finished the story, Lysevitch sat down on the sofa, exhausted.

"How splendid you are! How handsome!" he began, a little while afterward in a faint voice as if he were ill. "I am happy near you, dear girl, but why am I forty-two instead of thirty? Your tastes and mine do not coincide: you ought to be depraved, and I have long passed that phase, and want a love as delicate and immaterial as a ray of sunshine—that is, from the point of view of a woman of your age, I am of no earthly use."

In his own words, he loved Turgenev, the singer of virginal love and purity, of youth, and of the melancholy Russian landscape, but he loved virginal love, not from knowledge but from hearsay, as something abstract, existing outside real life. Now he assured himself that he loved Anna Akimovna platonically, ideally, though he did not know what those words meant. But he felt comfortable, snug, warm. Anna Akimovna seemed to him enchanting, original, and he imagined that the pleasant sensation that was aroused in him by these surroundings was the very thing that was called platonic love.

He laid his cheek on her hand and said in the tone commonly used in coaxing little children:

"My precious, why have you punished me?"

"How? When?"

"I have had no Christmas present from you."

Anna Akimovna had never heard before of their sending a Christmas box to the lawyer, and now she was at a loss how much to give him. But she must give him something, for he was expecting it, though he looked at her with eyes full of love.

"I suppose Nazaritch forgot it," she said, "but it is not too late to set it right."

She suddenly remembered the fifteen hundred she had received the day before, which was now lying in the toilet drawer in her bedroom. And when she brought that ungrateful money and gave it to the lawyer, and he put it in his coat pocket with indolent grace, the whole incident passed off charmingly and naturally. The sudden reminder of a Christmas gift and this fifteen hundred was not unbecoming in Lysevitch.

"*Merci*," he said, and kissed her finger.

Krylin came in with a blissful, sleepy face, but without his decorations.

Lysevitch and he stayed a little longer and drank a glass of tea each, and began to get ready to go. Anna Akimovna was a little embarrassed ... She had utterly forgotten in what department Krylin served, and whether she had to give him money or not; and if she had to, whether to give it now or send it afterwards in an envelope.

"Where does he serve?" she whispered to Lysevitch.

"Goodness knows," muttered Lysevitch, yawning.

She reflected that if Krylin used to visit her father and her uncle and respected them, it was probably not for nothing: apparently he had been charitable at their expense, serving in some charitable institution. As she said goodbye she slipped three hundred rubles into his hand; he seemed taken aback, and looked at her for a minute in silence with his pewter eyes, but then seemed to understand and said:

"The receipt, honored Anna Akimovna, you can only receive on the New Year."

Lysevitch had become utterly limp and heavy, and he staggered when Mishenka put on his overcoat.

As he went downstairs he looked like a man in the last stage of exhaustion, and it was evident that he would drop asleep as soon as he got into his sled.

"Your Excellency," he said languidly to Krylin, stopping in the middle of the staircase, "has it ever happened to you to experience a feeling as though some unseen force were drawing you out longer and longer? You are drawn out and turn into the finest wire. Subjectively this finds expression in a curious voluptuous feeling which is impossible to compare with anything."

Anna Akimovna, standing at the top of the stairs, saw each of them give Mishenka a note.

"Good-bye! Come again!" she called to them, and ran into her bedroom.

She quickly threw off her dress, which she was weary of already, put on a dressing gown, and ran downstairs. And as she ran downstairs she laughed and thumped with her feet like a schoolboy. She had a great desire for mischief.

IV

Evening

Auntie, in a loose print blouse, Varvarushka, and two old women were sitting in the dining room having supper. A big piece of salt meat, a ham, and various savories were lying on the table before them, and clouds of steam were rising from the meat, which looked particularly fatty and appetizing. Wine was not served on the lower story, but they made up for it with a great number of spirits and homemade liqueurs. Agafyushka, the fat, white-skinned, well-fed cook, was standing with her arms crossed in the doorway and talking to the old women, and the dishes were being served by the downstairs Masha, a dark girl with a crimson ribbon in her hair. The old women had had enough to eat before the morning was over, and an hour before supper they'd had tea and buns, and so they were now eating with effort—as it were, from a sense of duty.

"Oh, my girl!" sighed Auntie, as Anna Akimovna ran into the dining room and sat down beside her. "You've frightened me to death!"

Everyone in the house was pleased when Anna Akimovna was in good spirits and played pranks. This always reminded them that the old men were dead and that the old women had no authority in the house, and anyone could do as he liked without any fear of being sharply called to account for it. Only the two old women glanced askance at Anna Akimovna with amazement: she was humming, and it was a sin to sing at table.

"Our mistress, our beauty, our picture," Agafyushka began chanting with sugary sweetness. "Our precious jewel! The people, the people that have come today to look at our queen. Lord have mercy upon us! Generals, and officers and gentlemen … I kept looking out the window and counting and counting till I gave it up."

"I'd as soon they did not come at all," said Auntie. She looked sadly at her niece and added, "They only waste the time for my poor orphan girl."

Anna Akimovna felt hungry, as she had eaten nothing since the morning. They poured her out some very bitter liqueur; she drank it off, and tasted the salt meat with mustard, and thought it extraordinarily nice. Then the downstairs Masha brought in the turkey, the pickled apples, and the gooseberries. And that pleased her, too. There was only one thing that was disagreeable: there was a draft of hot air from the tiled stove; it was stiflingly close and everyone's cheeks were burning. After supper the cloth was taken off and plates of peppermint biscuits, walnuts, and raisins were brought in.

"You sit down, too, no need to stand there!" said Auntie to the cook.

Agafyushka sighed and sat down to the table. Masha set a wineglass of liqueur before her, too, and Anna Akimovna began to feel as though Agafyushka's white neck were giving out heat like the stove. They were all talking of how difficult it was nowadays to get married, and saying that in old days, if men did not court beauty, they paid attention to money, but now there was no making out what they wanted, and while hunchbacks and cripples used to be left old maids, nowadays men would not have even the beautiful and wealthy. Auntie began to set this down to immorality, and said that people had no fear of God, but she suddenly remembered that Ivan Ivanitch, her brother, and Varvarushka—both people of holy life—had feared God, but all the same had children on the sly, and had sent them to the Foundling Asylum. She pulled herself up and changed the conversation, telling them about a suitor she had once had, a factory hand, and how she had loved him, but her brothers had forced her to marry a widower, an icon painter, who, thank God, had died two years after. The downstairs Masha sat down to the table, too, and told them with a mysterious air that for the last week some unknown man with a black moustache, in a greatcoat with an astrakhan collar, had made his appearance every morning in the yard, had stared at the windows of the big house, and had gone on farther—to the buildings. The man was all right, nice-looking.

All this conversation made Anna Akimovna suddenly long to be married—long intensely, painfully; she felt as though she would give half her life and all her fortune only to know that upstairs there was a man who was closer to her than anyone in the world, that he loved her warmly and was missing her. The thought of such closeness, ecstatic and inexpressible in words, troubled her soul. And the instinct of youth and health flattered her with lying assurances that the real poetry of life was not over but still to come, and she believed it, and leaning back in her chair—her hair fell down as she did so—she began laughing, and, looking at her, the others laughed, too. And it was a long time before this causeless laughter died down in the dining room.

She was informed that the Stinging Beetle had come. This was a pilgrim woman called Pasha or Spiridonovna—a thin little woman of fifty, in a black dress with a white kerchief, with keen eyes, sharp nose, and a sharp chin. She had sly, viperish eyes and she looked as though she could see right through everyone. Her lips were shaped like a heart. Her viperishness and hostility to everyone had earned her the nickname of the Stinging Beetle.

Going into the dining room without looking at anyone, she made for the icons and chanted "Thy Holy Birth" in a high voice, then she sang "The Virgin Today Gives Birth to the Son," then "Christ is Born," then she turned around and bent a piercing gaze upon all of them.

"A happy Christmas," she said, and she kissed Anna Akimovna on the shoulder. "It's all I could do, all I could do to get to you, my kind friends." She kissed Auntie on the shoulder. "I should have come to you this morning, but I went in to some good people to rest on the way. 'Stay, Spiridonovna, stay,' they said, and I did not notice that evening was coming on."

As she did not eat meat, they gave her salmon and caviar. She ate looking from under her eyelids at the company, and drank three glasses of vodka. When she had finished she said a prayer and bowed down to Anna Akimovna's feet.

They began to play a game of "Kings," as they had done the year before, and the year before that, and all the servants in both stories crowded in at the doors to watch the game. Anna Akimovna fancied she caught a glimpse once or twice of Mishenka, with a patronizing smile on his face, among the crowd of peasant men and women. The first to be king was Stinging Beetle, and Anna Akimovna as the soldier paid her tribute; and then Auntie was king and Anna Akimovna was peasant, which excited general delight, and Agafyushka was prince, and was quite abashed with pleasure. Another game was got up at the other end of the table—played by the two Mashas, Varvarushka, and the sewing-maid, Marfa Petrovna, who was waked on purpose to play Kings, and whose face looked cross and sleepy.

While they were playing they talked of men, and of how difficult it was to get a good husband nowadays, and which state was to be preferred—that of an old maid or a widow.

"You are a pretty, healthy, sturdy lass," said Stinging Beetle to Anna Akimovna. "But I can't make out for whose sake you are holding back."

"What's to be done if nobody will have me?"

"Or maybe you have taken a vow to remain a maid?" Stinging Beetle went on, as though she did not hear. "Well, that's a good deed … Remain one," she repeated, looking intently and maliciously at her cards. "All right, my dear, remain one … Yes … only maids, these saintly maids, are not all alike." She heaved a sigh and played the king. "Oh, no, my girl, they are not all alike! Some really watch over themselves like nuns, and butter would not melt in their mouths, and if such a one does sin in an hour of weakness, she is worried to death, poor thing! So it would be a sin to condemn her. While others will go dressed in black and sew their shroud, and yet love rich old men on the sly. Yes, ye-es, my canary birds, some hussies will bewitch an old man and rule over him, my doves, rule over him and turn his head, and when they've saved up money and lottery tickets enough, they will bewitch him to his death."

Varvarushka's only response to these hints was to heave a sigh and look toward the icons. There was an expression of Christian meekness on her countenance.

"I know a maid like that, my bitterest enemy," Stinging Beetle went on, looking around at everyone in triumph. "She is always sighing, too, and looking at the icons, the she-devil. When she used to rule in a certain old man's house, if one went to her she would give one a crust, and bid bow down to the icons while she would sing: 'In Conception Thou Dost Abide A Virgin!' On holidays she will give one a bite, and on working days she will reproach one for it. But nowadays I will make merry over her! I will make as merry as I please, my jewel."

Varvarushka glanced at the icons again and crossed herself.

"But no one will have me, Spiridonovna," said Anna Akimovna to change the conversation. "What's to be done?"

"It's your own fault. You keep waiting for highly educated gentlemen, but you ought to marry one of your own sort, a merchant."

"We don't want a merchant," said Auntie, all in a flutter. "Queen of Heaven, preserve us! A gentleman will spend your money, but then he will be kind to you, you poor little fool. But a merchant will be so strict that you won't feel at home in your own house. You'll be wanting to fondle him and he will be counting his money, and when you sit down to meals with him, he'll begrudge you every mouthful, though it's your own, the lout! Marry a gentleman."

They all talked at once, loudly interrupting one another, and Auntie tapped on the table with the nutcrackers and said, flushed and angry:

"We won't have a merchant; we won't have one! If you choose a merchant I shall go to an almshouse."

"Sh … Sh! … Hush!" cried Stinging Beetle, and when all were silent she screwed up one eye and said: "Do you know what, Annushka, my birdie? There is no need for you to get married really like everyone else. You're rich and free, you are your own mistress; but yet, my child, it doesn't seem the right thing for you to be an old maid. I'll find you, you know, some trumpery and simple-witted man. You'll marry him for appearances and then fly away, ladybird! You can hand him five thousand or ten maybe, and pack him off where he came from, and you will be mistress in your own house—you can love whom you like and no one can say anything to you. And then you can love your highly educated gentleman. You'll have a jolly time!" Stinging Beetle snapped her fingers and gave a whistle.

"It's sinful," said Auntie.

"Oh, sinful," laughed Stinging Beetle. "She is educated, she understands. To cut someone's throat or bewitch an old man—that's a sin, that's true; but to love some charming young friend is not a sin at all. And what is there in it, really? There's no sin in it at all! The old pilgrim women have invented all that to make fools of simple folk. I, too, say everywhere it's a sin; I don't know myself why it's a sin." Stinging Beetle emptied her glass and cleared her throat. "Fly away, ladybird," this time evidently addressing herself. "For thirty years, wenches, I have thought of nothing but sins and been afraid, but now I see I have wasted my time, I've let it slip by like a ninny! Ah, I have been a fool, a fool!" She sighed. "A woman's time is short and every day is precious. You are pretty, Annushka, and very rich; but as soon as thirty-five or forty strikes for you your time is up. Don't listen to anyone, my girl—live, have your fun till you are forty, and then you will have time to pray forgiveness. There will be plenty of time to bow down and to sew your shroud. A candle to God and a poker to the devil! You can do both at once! Well, how is it to be? Will you make some little man happy?"

"I will," laughed Anna Akimovna. "I don't care now, I would marry a workingman."

"Well, that would do all right! Oh, what a fine fellow you would choose then!" Stinging Beetle screwed up her eyes and shook her head. "O-o-oh!"

"I tell her myself," said Auntie, "it's no good waiting for a gentleman, so she had better marry, not a gentleman, but someone humbler. Anyway we should have a man in the house to look after things. And there are lots of good men. She might have someone out of the factory. They are all sober, steady men …"

"I should think so," Stinging Beetle agreed. "They are capital fellows. If you like, Aunt, I will make a match for her with Vassily Lebedinsky?"

"Oh, Vasya's legs are so long," said Auntie seriously. "He is so lanky. He has no looks."

There was laughter in the crowd by the door.

"Well, Pimenov? Would you like to marry Pimenov?" Stinging Beetle asked Anna Akimovna.

"Very good. Make a match for me with Pimenov."

"Really?"

"Yes, do!" Anna Akimovna said resolutely, and she struck her fist on the table. "On my honor, I will marry him."

"Really?"

Anna Akimovna suddenly felt ashamed that her cheeks were burning and that everyone was looking at her. She flung the cards together on the table and ran out of the room. As she ran up the stairs and, reaching the upper story, sat down to the piano in the drawing room, a murmur of sound reached her from below like the roar of the sea—most likely they were talking of her and of Pimenov, and perhaps Stinging Beetle was taking advantage of her absence to insult Varvarushka and was putting no check on her language.

The lamp in the big room was the only light burning in the upper story, and it sent a glimmer through the door into the dark drawing room. It was between nine and ten, not later. Anna Akimovna played a waltz, then another, then a third; she went on playing without stopping. She looked into the dark corner beyond the piano, smiled, and inwardly called to it, and the idea occurred to her that she might drive off to the town to see someone, Lysevitch for instance, and tell him what was passing in her heart. She wanted to talk without ceasing, to laugh, to play the fool, but the dark corner was sullenly silent, and all around in all the rooms of the upper story it was still and desolate.

She was fond of sentimental songs, but she had a harsh, untrained voice, and so she played only the accompaniment and sang hardly audibly, just above her breath. She sang in a whisper one song after another, for the most part about love, separation, and frustrated hopes, and she imagined how she would hold out her hands to him and say with entreaty, with tears, "Pimenov, take this burden from me!" And then, just as though her sins had been forgiven, there would be joy and comfort in her soul, and perhaps a free, happy life would begin. In an anguish of anticipation she leaned over the keys, with a passionate longing for the change in her life to come at once without delay, and was terrified at the thought that her old life would go on for some time longer. Then she played again and sang hardly above her breath, and all was stillness about her. There was no noise coming from downstairs now, they must have gone to bed. It had struck ten some time before. A long, solitary, wearisome night was approaching.

Anna Akimovna walked through all the rooms, lay down for a while on the sofa, and read in her study the letters that had come that evening—there were twelve letters of Christmas greetings and three anonymous letters. In one of them some workman complained in a horrible, almost illegible handwriting that Lenten oil sold in the factory shop was rancid and smelt of paraffin; in another, someone respectfully informed her that over a purchase of iron Nazaritch had lately taken a bribe of a thousand rubles from someone; in a third she was abused for her inhumanity.

The excitement of Christmas was passing off, and to keep it up Anna Akimovna sat down at the piano again and softly played one of the new waltzes, then she remembered how cleverly and honestly she had spoken at dinner today. She looked round at the dark windows, at the walls with the pictures, at the faint light that came from the big room, and all at once she began suddenly crying, and she felt vexed that she was so lonely, and that she had no one to talk to and consult. To cheer herself she tried to picture Pimenov in her imagination, but it was unsuccessful.

It struck twelve. Mishenka, no longer wearing his swallowtail but in his reefer jacket, came in, and without speaking lighted two candles; then he went out and returned a minute later with a cup of tea on a tray.

"What are you laughing at?" she asked, noticing a smile on his face.

"I was downstairs and heard the jokes you were making about Pimenov—" he said, and put his hand before his laughing mouth. "If he were sat down to dinner today with Viktor Nikolaevitch and the general, he'd have died of fright." Mishenka's shoulders were shaking with laughter. "He doesn't know even how to hold his fork, I bet."

The footman's laughter and words, his reefer jacket and moustache, gave Anna Akimovna a feeling of uncleanness. She shut her eyes to avoid seeing him, and, against her own will, imagined Pimenov dining with Lysevitch and Krylin, and his timid, unintellectual figure seemed to her pitiful and helpless, and she felt repelled by it. And only now, for the first time in the whole day, she realized clearly that all she had said and thought about Pimenov and marrying a workman was nonsense, folly, and stupid willfulness. To convince herself of the opposite, to overcome her repulsion, she tried to recall what she had said at dinner, but now she could not see anything in it: shame at her own thoughts and actions, and the fear that she had said something improper during the day, and disgust at her own lack of spirit, overwhelmed her completely. She took up a candle and, as rapidly as if someone were pursuing her, ran downstairs, woke Spiridonovna, and began assuring her she had been joking. Then she went to her bedroom. Red-haired Masha, who was dozing in an armchair near the bed, jumped up and began shaking up the pillows. Her face was exhausted and sleepy, and her magnificent hair had fallen on one side.

"Tchalikov came again this evening," she said, yawning, "but I did not dare to announce him. He was very drunk. He says he will come again tomorrow."

"What does he want with me?" said Anna Akimovna, and she flung her comb on the floor. "I won't see him, I won't."

She made up her mind she had no one left in life but this Tchalikov, that he would never leave off persecuting her, and would remind her every day how uninteresting and absurd her life was. So all she was fit for was to help the poor. Oh, how stupid it was!

She lay down without undressing, and sobbed with shame and depression: what seemed to her most vexing and stupid of all was that her dreams that day about Pimenov had been right, lofty, honorable, but at the same time she felt that Lysevitch and even Krylin were nearer to her than Pimenov and all the workers taken together. She thought that if the long day she had just spent could have been represented in a picture, all that had been bad and vulgar—as, for instance, the dinner, the lawyer's talk, the game of Kings—would have been true, while her dreams and talk about Pimenov would have stood out from the whole as something false, as out of a drawing; and she thought, too, that it was too late to dream of happiness, that everything was over for her, and it was impossible to go back to the life when she had slept under the same quilt with her mother, or to devise some new special sort of life.

Red-haired Masha was kneeling before the bed, gazing at her in mournful perplexity; then she, too, began crying, and laid her face against her mistress's arm, and without words it was clear why she was so wretched.

"We are fools!" said Anna Akimovna, laughing and crying. "We are fools! Oh, what fools we are!"

1893

A DISTANT CHRISTMAS EVE

Klaudia Lukashevich

A frosty day. From the window, one can see the fluffy white snow covering the streets, the roofs of homes, and the trees. An early twilight. The sky is turning blue.

Lida and I are standing by the window, looking at the sky.

"Nanny, is the star coming soon?" I ask.

"Soon, soon," the old woman answers hurriedly. She is setting the table.

"Nanny, look, the star's come in the sky," Lida says happily.

"That's not it."

"Why isn't that it? Look real good."

"The right one will be bigger … This one's very small," says Nanny, barely glancing out the window.

"You said, 'Before the first star,'" says my sister tearfully.

"We haven't eaten a thing. We're starved," I add.

"Give them a little something to snack on … You've completely starved the girls." Mama heard our conversation, came out of her room, and gives us a big kiss.

"What you've thought up! Really, one can't eat before the first star. The entire day we've been fasting. And suddenly—they can't do it anymore. It's sinful," says Nanny gravely.

We also believe it's sinful—we'll be having *kutia*—the special holiday meal. One must wait for it. The adults fast the entire day and don't eat until the first star. We've decided to fast, like the grownups … but we're so awfully hungry and we repeat impatiently, "Oh, if only twilight would come quicker."

Nanny and Mama have set the table with a clean tablecloth and have laden it with straw. We like this very much. We know that this is done in remembrance of that greatest event: Our Lord was born in a cave and laid in a manger upon the hay.

We haven't eaten, as we usually do, at three o'clock, and we'll eat "with the star", that is, when it gets dark and the first star begins to burn in the sky. We will have kutia with rice, with almonds, wheat with honey and various holiday fish dishes. Besides all that, on top of the table are ears of wheat and oats.

For us children, this all seemed important and meaningful. Our apartment was spic and span and the lamps burned everywhere; the mood was one of reverence, with a whole day of fasting and the kutia which we only had once a year—everything hinted at the coming of a most important holiday … Nanny, of course, reminded us several times that "the Magi brought the holy frankincense, myrrh, gold, and wheat." That's the reason for eating wheat on Christmas Eve.

Our father was from Little Russia, and many customs were followed according to his practice. Somewhere far away on a small farm in the Poltavsky region lived his mother and sister and brother. And there they celebrated their Ukrainian holiday supper and ate their kutia. Papa told us all of this and loved the custom. But in the small gray building where Grandmother and Grandfather lived, they always ate kutia on Christmas Eve, too ... And they, and we too, always invited a lonely guest or guests on this evening: Grandfather's colleague or Papa's friend, who had nowhere to greet the holiday.

After making the kutia, we departed for evening vespers. But my sister and I were anxious: we are waiting for something out of the ordinary, something merry. And how is it possible not to be anxious? Christmas has arrived. Maybe we'll have a tree … What child's heart would not beat joyfully at such remembrances? The high holiday of Christmas, enveloped in sacred poetry, is especially clear and close to a child … The Holy Infant is born, praise and glory be to Him, may the world honor Him. Everyone exulted and rejoiced. And in commemoration of the baby Jesus on these days of holy remembrance, all children must make merry and rejoice. This is their day, the holiday of innocent, pure childhood.

And now it appears—a shapely green tree, to which so many legends and recollections are tied … Hello, you sweet, beloved Christmas tree! In the midst of winter you bring us the evergreen smell of the forests and, drenched in little lights, you delight the children's gaze, just as according to ancient legend you brought joy to the heavenly gaze of the Holy Infant. Our family had a custom for major holidays to make each other presents, surprises, to unexpectedly bring great happiness and joy. Each quietly prepared his handmade gift; we memorized poems; for the New Year and for Easter we placed the handmade present under our napkins ... We were engrossed in this tradition and it brought us much happiness. The gifts were simple, inexpensive, but they caused great delight.

The tree always seemed like a surprise, unexpected, and our parents, the nanny and aunts would decorate it while we slept.

Two or three days before Christmas mother would sadly announce, "Poor children, now you won't have a tree this year. Papa and I have no money. And Christmas trees are expensive. Next year we'll pick a great big one for you. But this year we'll have to get by without a tree." There was nothing to say to these words. But in the disappointed child's heart all the same there was concealed offense and a desperate hope. We believed and didn't believe the words of Mama and our loved ones.

On the first day of Christmas how many happy heads, children's heads, raise up from dreams with joyous visions in which a fir tree has been twinkling, how many naïve expectations pack full the childish imagination … And how happy and alluring it is to dream of the golden Christmas star, or some puppet, a drum, bright lights on the branches of a beloved little tree. All children have so many dreams, wishes, so many hopes connected with the holiday of Christmas.

"Lida, Lida, open your nose, it smells like a Christmas tree," I say, waking up on Christmas morning in the most happy mood. The ruddy, round face of my sister rises from the pillow. In a funny way she wrinkles her little nose.

"It does smell like one … It's true … It's almost as if it smells like one."

"And how could they say that there wouldn't be a tree this year?"

"Maybe there will be. Last year they also said we wouldn't have one, and then we had one after all," my sister recalls. Nanny is here in a jiffy.

"Nanny, what is it that smells so much like a tree?" I ask earnestly.

"How could it smell like a Christmas tree when there's not a trace of one? Get up, young lady, get up, little missy! The carolers are coming!"

"Are these Grandfather's 'children'?"

"Sure, with the star. Grandfather has glued it together for them."

"Of course, Grandfather, our joker, went to a lot of effort for his children ... I was at their place, the entire floor in the study is covered with a mess, as if gold has been shaken out everywhere. But the star is shining, it's shimmering. Do you see what I mean?"

In that faraway time there was a custom for carolers to visit apartments "with the star" and sing Christmas songs. As a rule, the local poor gathered in each home: the children and teenagers were taught Christmas songs, they crafted a star, and walked from home to home glorifying Christ. You barely had time to dress and wash up when Nanny would say, "They've come with the star." We would hear the rush of the children's feet and a group of six or ten people would come into the apartment. The children would stand before the icons and start singing, "Your Christmas" and "The Virgin Today." Then they'd boisterously wish you a merry Christmas. Sometimes the singing came out strong and beautiful. There was a touching and celebratory element in the appearance of the carolers. My sister and I were fond of the tradition, it delighted us, and we impatiently awaited the arrival of the carolers.

Revelers came several times on the first day of Christmas. Nobody was turned away empty-handed from our home: they conferred kopecks and *prianiki*—gingerbread cookies—on one and all. But we especially looked forward to the coming of Grandfather's "children." We would know them from thousands, they appeared with such a beautiful, elaborate star, such as nobody else could boast of. Our very own artist had made it—Grandfather. Even Nanny would tenderly say, "Here they are, Grandfather's children are coming."

We were frozen in anticipation. The group bashfully entered the room, and in front of them was a beautiful gold star. It sat on a long pole, surrounded by a golden halo—it trembled and shimmered. And in the middle was a picture of the birth of Christ.

"You see, Lida, that's where Christ was born," I point out to my sister, on the star.

"I see. Grandfather drew that. I know it."

It seemed to us that Grandfather's children sang especially loud and boisterously. The familiar, friendly faces of the "barefoot brigade," as we called them, smiled at my sister and me. And we were confused, and hid ourselves behind Nanny and Mama. Grandfather's children were given presents beyond those for others, more luxurious. They were even given *sbiten*, the hot honey drink. How happy they were, and how long they remembered this.

On the first day of Christmas our holiday mood was darkened a bit: we didn't know if there would be a tree or not.

"Mama says there won't be."

"Then why was she laughing?" I would say worriedly to my sisters. "She turned around and laughed."

"She always laughs …"

"Then why is the door to that room closed? And it smells like a Christmas tree!"

"Mama says there are coal fumes in there and they're airing out the room. It's cold in there."

The story about the fumes sounded like the truth and we would begin to believe it. We couldn't shake the nervous feeling. And we secretly consulted each other:

"You can peek through the crack."

"No, Nanny said we mustn't peek."

But the curiosity was so great that we fleetingly glanced through the crack and saw something beautiful, twinkling, green. It looked like a tree!

In my little corner we would already be playing, imitating the carolers, arranging a tree out of a small flower for the puppets. But when Grandmother and Grandfather came with our aunts, bearing packages, hope would once again fill our hearts. Soon Aunt Manyusha would busy us with a story. We'd listen and forget temporarily about the tree. Then Mama would begin to sing a joyful song, and lead us grandly into the closed room. The door swung open—and the lights on the tree were shining. I don't know if this ancient custom of unexpectedly enlivening the children with the tree is a good one. The ecstasy was so strong that happiness put a stop to your breathing. You stood a while, mouth agape, and you couldn't speak a word. Your eyes sparkled, your cheeks went flush, and you weren't sure what you were seeing. Then Mother and Father would grab your hand and begin to circle around the tree with songs.

Our tree was modest, small, but so prettily decorated, with love. Under the tree were gifts. Everybody gave a gift to somebody else. The aunties had knitted us pinafores. Grandmother sewed us a little ball from rags. Papa and Grandfather had made benches; Mama drew pictures. Nanny had dressed our puppets. And we too had made gifts for everyone: poems, bookmarks, oversleeves. Everything was done with Nanny's help and guidance. The adults, especially Mama and the aunts, sang with us and danced around the tree. It was so joyous. But unfortunately, in early childhood there were no other children at our tree: we had no little friends. I remember Nanny once brought over the children of the washerwoman and sat them down before our tree. At first we thought that they were huge puppets. But when we looked again, it wasn't a reason for joy and jubilation. We didn't know how and what to play with our little friends, or what to give them. But a child after all is drawn to the group of his peers, to children's occupations and games with friends. And in the end it seemed that this, our tree, was happiest and most memorable when the children of the washerwoman were with us.

Grandfather's Christmas trees were much different. There were so many children there. "Papa is making such an effort for his children, and he doesn't even think about his grandchildren," Auntie Sasha said in an unhappy voice. But the grandchildren were in indescribable ecstasy over Grandfather's tree. In that small apartment in the gray building, to hide a tree would have been impossible—and we saw it beforehand: charming and decorated with elaborate twine, bulbs, stars and candy boxes. Grandfather had put them all on himself, and Papa and Mama helped him.

Besides the tree, we and the "barefoot brigade" of about twelve or fifteen children who gathered in Grandfather's study always waited for some surprise which would bring us joy and entertainment no less than the tree. Grandfather, the family joker, would do surprising things: he was a master of everything to do with his hands. "Will Grandfather put on a performance? What did he think up this time?" Lida and I would exclaim. We and the other guests were led into the kitchen, and in the study we could hear the whisper of impatient voices. Grandfather walked into the hallway and began to call us, first by ringing some bells, then with a whistle, then a rooster's crow. Afterward he sat at his fortepiano and played an old bombastic marching tune. He was the only one who knew it. Under this march, we were led into the kitchen, and the little ones—into the study. Mama or Papa usually led them there. All of us, with Grandfather's march in the background, surrounded the tree and sat on the arranged benches. Immediately, some sort of show would begin. Every year it was different: one day Grandfather built a puppet theater, and all the paper actors spoke in different voices; they bowed, sang, danced, like real people. Another time he showed us magic. While he did this, he wore a sharp-edged hat and black cloak with golden stars. The naïve viewers were wonderstruck at how, out of Grandfather's mouth, a dozen apples would come tumbling out, coins would fall from his nose, a handkerchief would disappear in his hands. We all thought he was a brilliant magician and wizard.

But best of all was when Grandfather would set up his Laterna Magica. With the help of our father he made a beautiful magic lamp, and he drew a heap of pictures on the glass: swirling stars, little demons jumping over each other, a nose on an old man that grew to incredible proportions. At the same time, Grandfather supplemented all the pictures with stories and rhymes and jokes: while he showed us a thin little girl on the screen, he would say: "This is little Sofia, three years on the stove she napped, got up, made a bow, into pieces she snapped. Wanted to put her together but she was shakier than a feather. I wanted to make her right, her legs just wouldn't take flight. Picked her up with the needle to sew … and gently let her go.

Everyone doubled over in laughter, of course, especially the little ones.

After the show there were celebrations around the lit tree. Grandfather played his march, and the folks moved around and even danced. I remember that everybody, including us, drank hot sbiten and enjoyed a treat. Toward the end there was a special number, and Grandmother and the aunts always were against it. And we were strictly forbidden to participate. But we enjoyed it and were fascinated, and we envied them that we couldn't take part. They extinguished the tree; Grandfather tipped it over onto the floor and shouted, "Gather it up, children!" Then a scuffle began immediately, and shouting and noise. We all jumped on the tree and picked it clean of its last prianik. And then, with laughter, we dragged it into the courtyard and even stripped it of its branches.

Grandfather was very joyful and happy with his barefoot brigade. He turned into a child himself: he sang, joked, frolicked, played his march. What a shining light that holiday was, in the little gray building, for those children of bitter poverty, who gathered at the tree of their "guide." They dreamed of the tree all year and it shined ever brighter than the Christmas star which Grandfather had made for them, and which he used to glorify Christ.

1917

THE LITTLE BOY AT CHRIST'S CHRISTMAS TREE

Fyodor Dostoevsky

I

In a large city, on Christmas Eve in the biting cold, I see a young child, still quite young, six years old, perhaps even less; too young yet to be sent on the street begging, but assuredly destined to be sent in a year or two.

This child awakes one morning in a damp and frosty cellar. He is wrapped in a kind of squalid dressing gown and is shivering. His breath issues from between his lips in white vapor. He is seated on a trunk; to pass the time he blows the breath from his mouth, and amuses himself in seeing it escape. But he is very hungry. Several times since morning he has drawn near the bed covered with a straw mattress as thin as gauze, where his mother lies sick, her head resting on a bundle of rags instead of a pillow.

How did she come there? She came probably from a strange city and has fallen ill. The proprietress of the miserable lodging was arrested two days ago, and carried to the police station. It is a holiday today, and the other tenants have gone out. However, one of them has remained in bed for the last twenty-four hours, stupid with drink, not having waited for the holiday.

From another corner issue the complaints of an old woman of eighty years, laid up with rheumatism. This old woman was formerly a children's nurse somewhere; now she is dying all alone. She whines, moans, and growls at the little boy, who begins to be afraid to come near the corner where she lies with the death rattle in her throat. He has found something to drink in the hallway, but he has not been able to lay his hand on the smallest crust of bread, and for the tenth time he comes to wake his mother. He finishes by getting frightened in this darkness.

The evening is already late, and no one comes to kindle the fire. He finds, by feeling around, his mother's face, and is astonished that she no longer moves and that she has become as cold as the wall.

"It is so terribly cold!" he thinks.

He remains some time without moving, his hand resting on the shoulder of the corpse. Then he begins to blow on his fingers to warm them, and, happening to find his little cap on the bed, he looks softly for the door, and issues forth from the underground lodging.

He would have gone out sooner had he not been afraid of the big dog that barks all the day up there on the landing at the neighbor's door.

Oh, what a city! Never before had he seen anything like it. Down yonder from where he came, the nights are much darker. There is only one lamp for the whole street, little low wooden houses, closed with shutters, and in the street from the time it grows dark there is no one about. Everyone's shut up at home. There is only a crowd of dogs that howl, hundreds, thousands of dogs that howl and bark all the night. But then, it used to be so warm there! And he got something to eat. Here, ah! How good it would be to have something to eat! What noise here, what an uproar! What great light, and what a crowd of people! What horses, and what carriages! And the cold, the cold! The bodies of the tired horses smoke with frost and their burning nostrils puff white clouds; their shoes ring on the pavement through the soft snow. And how everybody hustles everybody else! "Ah! how I would like to eat a little piece of something. That is what makes my fingers ache so."

II

A policeman just passes by, and turns his head so as not to see the child.

"Here is another street. Oh, how wide it is! I shall be crushed to death here, I know. How they all shout, how they run, how they roll along! And the light, and the light! And that, what is that? What a big window! And behind the window, a room, and in the room a tree that goes up to the ceiling. It is the Christmas tree. And what lights under the tree! Such papers of gold, and such apples! And all around dolls and little hobby horses. There are little children well dressed, nice, and clean; they are laughing and playing, eating and drinking things. There is a little girl going to dance with the little boy. How pretty she is! And there is music. I can hear it through the glass."

The child looks, admires, and even laughs. He no longer feels any pain in his fingers or feet. The fingers of his hand have become all red, he cannot bend them any more, and it hurts him to move them. But all at once, he feels that his fingers ache; he begins to cry, and moves along. He perceives through another window another room, and again trees and cakes of all sorts on the table, red almonds and yellow ones. Four beautiful ladies are sitting down, and when anybody comes in he is given some cake, and the door opens every minute, and many gentlemen enter. The little fellow crept forward, opened the door of a sudden, and went in. What noise was made when they saw him, what confusion! Immediately a lady arose, put a kopeck in his hand, and opened the door to the street for him. He was so frightened.

III

The kopeck has fallen from his hands, and rings on the steps of the stairs. He was not able to tighten his little fingers enough to hold the coin. The child went out running, and walked fast, fast. Where was he going? He did not know. And he runs, runs, and blows in his hands. He is troubled. He feels so lonely, so frightened. And suddenly, what is that again? A crowd of people stand there and admire. A window! Behind the window, three pretty dolls attired in wee red and yellow dresses, exactly as though they were alive! And that little old man sitting down, who seems to play the fiddle. There are two others, too, standing up, who play on tiny violins, keeping time with their heads to the music. They look at each other and their lips move. And do they really speak? Only they cannot be heard through the glass.

And the child first thinks that they are living, and when he comprehends that they are only dolls, he begins to laugh. Never had he seen such dolls before, and he didn't know that there were any like that! He would like to cry, but those dolls are just too funny!

IV

Suddenly he feels himself seized by the coat. A big rough boy stands near him, gives him a blow of his fist on the head, snatches his cap, and trips him up.

The child falls. At the same time there is a shout; he remains a moment paralyzed with fear. Then he springs up with a bound and runs, runs, darts under a gateway somewhere and hides himself in a courtyard behind a pile of wood. He cowers and shivers in his fright. He can hardly breathe.

And suddenly he feels quite comfortable. His little hands and feet don't hurt any more. He is warm, warm as though near a stove, and all his body trembles. It's as if he's gone to sleep.

"Ah, how nice it is to have a nap! I shall stay a little while and then I will go and see the dolls again," thought the little fellow, and he smiled at the recollection of the dolls. "They looked just as though they were alive!"

Then he hears his mother's song. "Mama, I am going to sleep. Ah, how nice it is here for sleeping!"

"Come to my house, little boy, to see the Christmas tree," said a soft voice.

He thought at first it was his mother; but no, it was not her.

Then who is calling him? He does not see. But someone stoops over him, and folds him in his arms in the darkness. He stretches out his hand and—all at once—Oh! What light! What a Christmas tree! No, it is not a Christmas tree; he has never seen the like of it!

Where is he now? All is resplendent, all is radiant, and dolls all around; but no, not dolls, little boys, little girls, only they are very bright. All of them circle around him. They fly. They hug him, they take him and carry him away, and he is flying too. And he sees his mother looking at him and laughing joyfully.

"Mama, Mama! How nice it is here!" cries her little boy to her.

And again he embraces the children, and would like very much to tell them about the dolls behind the windowpane. "Who are you, little girls?" he asks, laughing and caressing them.

"This is the Christmas tree at Jesus's," they answer him." At Jesus's, on this day, there is always a Christmas tree for little children that have none themselves."

And he learned that all these little boys and girls were children like himself, who had died like him. Some had died of cold in the baskets abandoned at the doors of the public functionaries of St. Petersburg; others had died out at nurse in the foul hovels of the Finns; others of hunger at the dry breasts of their mothers during the famine. All are here now, all little angels now, all with Jesus, and He Himself among them, spreading His hands over them, blessing them and their sinful mothers.

And the mothers of these children are there too, apart, weeping. Each recognizes her son or her daughter, and the children fly towards them, embrace them, wipe away the tears with their little hands, and beg them not to weep.

And below, on the earth, the custodian in the morning found the wee corpse of the child, who had taken refuge in the courtyard. Stiff and frozen behind the pile of wood it lay.

The mother was found too. She died before him. Both are reunited in Heaven in the Lord's house.

1876

CHRISTMAS PHANTOMS

Maxim Gorky

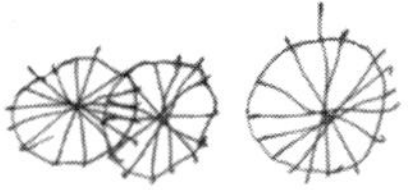

My Christmas story was concluded. I flung down my pen, rose from the desk, and began to pace up and down the room.

It was night, and outside the snowstorm whirled through the air. Strange sounds reached my ears as of soft whispers, or of sighs, that penetrated from the street through the walls of my little chamber, three-fourths of which were engulfed in dark shadows. It was the snow driven by the wind that came crunching against the walls and lashed the windowpanes. A light, white, indefinite object scurried past my window and disappeared, leaving a cold shiver within my soul.

I approached the window, looked out upon the street, and leaned my head, heated with the strained effort of imagination, upon the cold frame. The street lay in deserted silence. Now and then the wind ripped up little transparent clouds of snow from the pavement and sent them flying through the air like shreds of a delicate white fabric. A lamp burned opposite my window. Its flame trembled and quivered in fierce struggle with the wind. The flaring streak of light projected like a broadsword into the air, and the snow that was drifted from the roof of the house into this streak of light became aglow for a moment like a scintillating robe of sparks. My heart grew sad and chill as I watched this play of the wind. I quickly undressed myself, put out the lamp, and lay down to sleep.

When the light was extinguished and darkness filled my room, the sounds grew more audible and the window stared at me like a great white spot. The ceaseless ticking of the clock marked the passing of the seconds. At times their swift onward rush was drowned in the wheezing and crunching of the snow, but soon I heard again the low beat of the seconds as they dropped into eternity. Occasionally their sound was as distinct and precise as if the clock stood in my own skull.

I lay in my bed and thought of the story that I had just completed, wondering whether it had come out a success.

In this story I told of two beggars, a blind old man and his wife, who in silent, timid retirement trod the path of life that offered them nothing but fear and humiliation. They had left their village on the morning before Christmas to collects alms in the neighboring settlements that they might on the day thereafter celebrate the birth of Christ in holiday fashion.

They expected to visit the nearest villages and to be back home for the early morning service, with their bags filled with all kinds of crumbs doled out to them for the sake of Christ.

Their hopes (thus I proceeded in my narration) were naturally disappointed. The gifts they received were scanty, and it was very late when the pair, worn out with the day's tramp, finally decided to return to their cold, desolate clay hut. With light burdens on their shoulders and with heavy grief in their hearts, they slowly trudged along over the snow-covered plain, the old woman walking in front and the old man holding fast to her belt and following behind. The night was dark, clouds covered the sky, and for two old people the way to the village was still very long. Their feet sank into the snow and the wind whirled it up and drove it into their faces. Silently and trembling with cold, they plodded on and on. Weary and blinded by the snow, the old woman had strayed from the path, and they were now wandering aimlessly across the valley out on the open field.

"Are we going to be home soon? Take care that we do not miss the early mass!" mumbled the blind man behind his wife's shoulders.

She said that they would soon be home, and a new shiver of cold passed through her body. She knew that she had lost the way, but she dared not tell her husband. At times it seemed to her as if the wind carried the sound of the barking dogs to her ears, and she turned in the direction whence those sounds came; but soon she heard the barking from the other side.

At length her powers gave way and she said to the old man, "Forgive me, father, forgive me for the sake of Christ. I have strayed from the road and I cannot go further. I must sit down."

"You will freeze to death," he answered.

"Let me rest only for a little while. And even if we do freeze to death, what matters it? Surely our life on this earth is not sweet."

The old man heaved a heavy sigh and consented.

They sat down on the snow with their backs against each other and looked like two bundles of rags—the sport of the wind. It drifted clouds of snow against them, covered them up with sharp, pointed crystals, and the old woman, who was more lightly dressed than her husband, soon felt herself in the embrace of a rare, delicious warmth.

"Mother," called the blind man, who shivered with violent cold, "stand up, we must be going!"

But she had dozed off and muttered but half-intelligible words through her sleep. He endeavored to raise her, but he could not for want of adequate strength.

"You will freeze!" he shouted, and then he called aloud for help into the wide open field.

But she felt so warm, so comfortable! After some vain endeavor the blind man sat down again on the snow in dumb desperation. He was now firmly convinced that all that happened to him was by the express will of God and there was no escape for him and his aged wife. The wind whirled and danced around them in wanton frolic, playfully bestrewed them with snow and had a merry, roguish sport with the tattered garments that covered their old limbs, weary with a long life of pinching destitution. The old man also was now overcome with a feeling of delicious comfort and warmth.

Suddenly the wind wafted the sweet, solemn, melodious sounds of a bell to his ears.

"Mother!" he cried, starting back, "they are ringing for matins. Quick, let us go!"

But she had already gone whence there is no return.

"Do you hear? They are ringing, I say. Get up! Oh, we will be too late!"

He tried to rise, but he found that he could not move. Then he understood that his end was near and he began to pray silently: "Lord, be gracious unto the souls of your servants! We were sinners, both. Forgive us, O Lord! Have mercy upon us!"

Then it seemed to him that from across the field, enveloped in a bright, sparkling snow cloud, a radiant temple of God was floating toward him—a rare, wondrous temple. It was all made of flaming hearts of men and itself had the likeness of a heart, and in the midst of it, upon an elevated pedestal, stood Christ in his own person. At this vision the old man rose and fell upon his knees on the threshold of the temple. He regained his sight again and he looked at the Savior and Redeemer. And from his elevated position Christ spoke in a sweet, melodious voice: "Hearts aglow with pity are the foundation of my temple. Enter thou into my temple, thou who in thy life hast thirsted for pity, thou who has suffered misfortune and humiliation, go to thy Eternal Peace!"

"O Lord!" spoke the old man, restored to sight, weeping with rapturous joy, "is it Thou in truth O Lord!"

And Christ smiled benignly upon the old man and his life companion, who was awakened to life again by the smile of the Savior.

And thus both beggars froze to death out in the open snow-covered field.

I brought back to mind the various incidents of the story and wondered whether it had come out smooth and touching enough to arouse the reader's pity. It seemed to me that I could answer the question in the affirmative, that it could not possibly fail to produce the effect at which I had aimed.

With this thought I fell asleep, well satisfied with myself. The clock continued to tick, and I heard in my sleep the chasing and roaring of the snowstorm, that grew more and more violent. The lantern was blown out. The storm outside produced ever new sounds. The window shutters clattered. The branches of the trees near the door knocked against the metal plate of the roof. There was a sighing, groaning, howling, roaring, and whistling, and all this was now united into a woeful melody that filled the heart with sadness, now into a soft, low strain like a cradlesong. It had the effect of a fantastic tale that held the soul as if under a spell.

But suddenly—what was this? The faint spot of the window flamed up into a bluish phosphorescent light, and the window grew larger and larger until it finally assumed the proportions of the wall. In the blue light that filled the room there appeared of a sudden a thick white cloud in which bright sparks glowed as with countless eyes. As if whirled about by the wind, the cloud turned and twisted, began to dissolve, became more and more transparent, broke into tiny pieces, and breathed a frosty chill into my body that filled me with anxiety. Something like a dissatisfied angry mumble proceeded from the shreds of cloud that gained more and more definite shape and assumed forms familiar to my eye. Yonder in the corner were a swarm of children, or rather the shades of children, and behind them emerged a gray-bearded old man by the side of several female forms.

"Whence do these shades come? What do they wish?" were the questions that passed through my mind as I gazed affrighted at this strange apparition.

"Whence come we and whence are we?" was the solemn retort of a serious, stern voice. "Do you not know us? Think a little!"

I shook my head in silence. I did not know them. They kept floating through the air in rhythmic motion as if they led a solemn dance to the tune of the storm. Half transparent, scarcely discernible in their outlines, they wavered lightly and noiselessly around me, and suddenly I distinguished in their midst the blind old man who held on fast to the belt of his old wife. Deeply bent, they limped past me, their eyes fixed upon me with a reproachful look.

"Do you recognize them now?" asked the same solemn voice. I did not know whether it was the voice of the storm or the voice of my conscience, but there was in it a tone of command that brooked no contradiction.

"Yes, this is who they are," continued the Voice, "the sad heroes of your successful story. And all the others are also heroes of your Christmas stories—children, men, and women whom you made to freeze to death in order to amuse the public. See how many there are and how pitiful they look, the offspring of your fancy!"

A movement passed through the wavering forms and two children, a boy and a girl, appeared in the foreground. They looked like two flakes of snow or of the sheen of the moon.

"These children," spoke the Voice, "you have caused to freeze under the window of that rich house in which beamed the brilliant Christmas tree. They were looking at the tree—do you recollect—and they froze."

Noiselessly my poor little heroes floated past me and disappeared. They seemed to dissolve in the nebulous blue glare of light. In their place appeared a woman with a sorrowful, emaciated countenance.

"This is that poor woman who was hurrying to her village home on Christmas Eve to bring her children some cheap Christmas gifts. You have let her freeze to death also."

I gazed full of shame and fear at the shade of the woman. She also vanished, and new forms appeared in their turn. They were all sad, silent phantoms with an expression of unspeakable woe in their somber gaze.

And again I heard the solemn Voice speak in sustained, impassioned accents:

"Why have you written these stories? Is there not enough of real, tangible, and visible misery in the world that you must needs invent more misery and sorrow, and strain your imagination in order to paint pictures of thrilling, realistic effects? Why do you do this? What is your object? Do you wish to deprive man of all joy in life, do you wish to take from him the last drop of faith in the good by painting for him only the evil? Why is it that in your Christmas stories year after year you cause to freeze to death now children, now grown-up people? Why? What is your aim?"

I was staggered by this strange indictment. Everybody writes Christmas stories according to the same formula. You take a poor boy or a poor girl, or something of that sort, and let them freeze somewhere under a window, behind which there is usually a Christmas tree that throws its radiant splendor upon them. This has become the fashion, and I was following the fashion.

I answered accordingly.

"If I let these people freeze," I said, "I do it with the best object in the world. By painting their death struggle I stir up humane feelings in the public for these unfortunates. I want to move the heart of my reader, that is all."

A strange agitation passed through the throng of phantoms, as if they wished to raise a mocking protest against my words.

"Do you see how they are laughing?" said the mysterious Voice.

"Why are they laughing?" I asked in a scarcely audible tone.

"Because you speak so foolishly. You wish to arouse noble feelings in the hearts of men by your pictures of imagined misery, when real misery and suffering are nothing to them but a daily spectacle. Consider for how long a time people have endeavored to stir up noble feelings in the hearts of men, think of how many men before you have applied their genius to that end, and then take a look into real life! Fool that you are! If the reality does not move them, and if their feelings are not offended by its cruel, ruthless misery, and by the fathomless abyss of actual wretchedness, then how can you hope that the fictions of your imagination will make them better? Do you really think that you can move the heart of a human being by telling him about a frozen child? The sea of misery breaks against the dam of heartlessness, it rages and surges against it, and you want to appease it by throwing a few peas into it."

The phantoms accompanied these words with their silent laughter, and the storm laughed a shrill, cynical laugh; but the Voice continued to speak unceasingly. Each word that it spoke was like a nail driven into my brain. It became intolerable, and I could no longer hold out.

"It is all a lie, a lie!" I cried in a paroxysm of rage, and jumping from my bed, I fell headlong into the dark, and sank more and more quickly, more and more deeply, into the gaping abyss that suddenly opened before me. The whistling, howling, roaring, and laughing followed me downward, and the phantoms chased me through the dark, grinned in my face, and mocked at me.

I awoke in the morning with a violent headache and in a very bad humor. The first thing I did was to read over my story of the blind beggar and his wife once more, and then I tore the manuscript into pieces.

1896

A LIFELESS ANIMAL

Teffi

The Christmas party was lots of fun. There were many guests, grown-ups and little ones. There was even one boy who'd been whipped that day, Nanny kept whispering to Katya. This was so fascinating that Katya barely left his side the entire evening. She kept waiting for him to say something special, and she looked at him with respect and fear. But the boy who'd been whipped behaved himself in the most ordinary fashion, he asked before taking a gingerbread cookie, he blew the trumpet and horsed around with other boys, so that Katya, albeit reluctantly, eventually became disillusioned with him and moved away.

The evening was already coming to an end and the little ones, the ones crying loudly, were being dressed for outside, when Katya received her most important present—a great stuffed ram. He was all soft, with a long, meek face and human eyes, the smell of wet fur, and if you stretched his head downwards, he tenderly and persistently bleated out, "Me-eh."

The ram bewildered Katya with his look, his smell, his voice, and so, simply for peace of mind, she asked her mother, "Are you sure he's not alive?"

Her mother turned away her bird-like face and didn't say anything; for a long time now she hadn't answered Katya, she never had the time. Katya sighed and walked to the dining room to give the ram some milk. She thrust the ram's muzzle right into the saucer, until he was sopping wet all the way to his eyes. A young mistress whom she didn't know walked up to her and, shaking her head, said, "Ay-ay, what are you doing? Really now, you can't give a lifeless animal live milk to drink! You've got to give him phony milk. Like this."

She scooped her empty cup into the air, brought the glass to the ram's mouth, and wet his lips.

"Do you see?"

"I see. But why does the cat get real milk?"

"That's what the cat needs. Each animal has its own habits. For a living one—live milk. For a lifeless one—phony milk."

The woolen ram lived in the nursery, in the corner, behind Nanny's trunk. Katya loved him, and out of love she made him dirtier each day, and more tussled, and he said his "Me-eh" ever quieter. And because he'd grown so dirty, Mama didn't allow him to sit at table with them.

After supper, things were usually grim. Papa was silent, Mama was silent. Nobody even turned around after dessert when Katya curtsied and said in the thin voice of an intelligent girl, "*Merci, Papa. Merci, Mama.*"

Once, they sat down to supper without Mama. She returned home after they'd already had their soup and shouted from the entryway that there were so many people at the skating rink. And when she came to the table, Papa looked at her and abruptly smashed a decanter on the floor.

"What's wrong with you?"

He shouted something else, but Nanny scooped Katya up from the table and dragged her to the nursery.

After that Katya didn't see Papa or Mama for many days, and her entire life passed by in some unreal manner. They brought her the servants' meals from the kitchen; the cook would come in and she'd whisper with the nanny: "And he says to her … And she says to him … 'Why, you,' she says … 'Get out of here!' So she says … And he says ...

They whispered and spoke in hushed tones.

Some women with faces just like foxes began coming from the kitchen; they winked at Katya, they asked the nanny questions, they whispered and spoke in hushed tones:

"So he says to her … 'Ou-out!' And she says …"

The nanny often left the courtyard. Then the fox-faced women would gather in the nursery, they rooted around in the corners and waved their knotty fingers at Katya.

And when the women weren't there it was even worse. It was frightening.

She was forbidden to walk about in the large rooms; they were empty, they echoed. The curtains on the door billowed, the clock above the fireplace ticked gravely. And everywhere there was that: "So he says … So she says …"

Before supper the edges of the nursery grew darker, things stirred. And in the corner the furnace crackled—the daughter of the large stove, it jiggled its hatch, bared its red teeth, and devoured the kindling. One couldn't approach the stove—it was ill-tempered, it had bitten Katya on the finger. It no longer beckoned.

Everything was uneasy, nothing was as it had been before.

It was quiet only behind the trunk, where the woolly ram settled down, the lifeless animal. He snacked on pencils, old ribbon, Nanny's eyeglasses—God know's what, he accepted it, and gazed at Katya gently and tenderly; he never complained at all and understood everything.

One time she got up to mischief and the ram—she could tell—although he turned his face away, he laughed. And when Katya bandaged his neck with a rag when he was so pitifully sick, she herself cried quietly.

Nighttime it was even worse. All through the house there was scuttling and peeping. Katya would wake up and call for Nanny.

"Shoo! Sleep! The rats are scurrying about, by and by they'll bite off your nose!"

Katya stretched the blanket over her head, thought about her woolly lamb and when she felt him nearby, her very own, lifeless, close, she calmly fell asleep.

And once, in the morning, she and the ram were watching out the window. Suddenly they saw something brown and scampering, small, mangy, perhaps a cat, only with a longer tail.

"Nanny, Nanny! Look at that nasty cat!"

The nanny came up to the window and extended her neck.

"That's a rat, not a cat! A rat. Look, he's a big one. One like that could take out a cat in one fell swoop! It's a rat!"

She said these words with so much revulsion, expanding her mouth and baring her teeth like an old cat, that Katya felt her stomach turn inside out.

And the rat, swinging its belly, scurried to the neighbor's storehouse in a proprietary and businesslike manner, and sitting down, crept beneath the cellar door.

The cook came and said that the rats had increased so much in number that soon they'd bite her head off.

"In the storeroom they nibbled away all the corners of the master's suitcase. Brazen, are they! I walk in and the rat sits there and doesn't move a muscle."

The fox-like women came at night, they brought a bottle and some stinking fish. They snacked, sharing with the nanny, and then everyone started laughing for some reason.

"You're still busying yourself with that ram," said one of the fatter women to Katya. "Soon to the knackery, that one. He's lame in the leg and all mangy of wool. He's done for, your ram."

"Quit teasing her," the nanny butted in. "You don't pick on an orphan."

"I'm not teasing, I'm talking sense. The stuffing's coming out of him, and they'll finish him off. A living body eats and drinks, and that's why it's alive, but a rag, no matter how much you take him to the trough, all the same it'll go to pieces. And she's hardly an orphan, the one's mother probably drives by the house and laughs into her hand. Hee-hee-hee!"

The women were sopping with sweat from their laughter and Nanny dipped a cube of sugar into her glass and gave it Katya to suck on. The nanny's sugar scratched Katya's throat, her ears rang, and she tugged at the ram's head.

"He's not stupid: He makes his sound, do you hear?"

"Hee-hee! Ah, you stupid girl!" sniggered the fat woman once again. "You tug the door and it makes a sound, too. If it was a real ram, he'd go grazing."

The women drank another glass and began speaking the old words in a whisper:

"And he said … 'Ou-out' … And she said …"

But Katya went behind the trunk with the ram and began agonizing.

No life left in that ram. He'd die. The stuffing would fall out, and kaput. If she could only get him to eat, just a little!

She took down the sugar from the windowsill, stuck it right under his nose, and turned away, so as not to embarrass him. Perhaps he'd just take a little bite. She waited, turned back—no, the sugar was untouched.

"If I start eating myself, then maybe he'll feel more comfortable."

She bit off the tip of the cube, offered it to the ram again, turned around, and waited. Again, the ram didn't take a bite of the sugar.

"Why not? Can't you? You're not alive, and you can't!"

But the woolly ram, the lifeless animal, answered with his whole meek and sad face, "I can't! I'm not a living animal, I can't!"

"Come on, call to me yourself. Say, 'Me-eh.' Come on. 'Me-eh.' Can't you? You can't!"

And out of pity and love for the poor lifeless animal her heart was so sweetly broken in two. Katya fell asleep on the pillow wet with tears and immediately she was walking along an overgrown path, the ram was walking beside her, munching on grass, bleating all by himself, calling out, and laughing. Ah, he was so healthy, he could survive everything!

The morning was tedious, dark, unsettled and unexpectedly Papa appeared. He arrived all gray and angry, his beard was untrimmed, he peered out frowning, angry as a goat. He thrust out his hand for Katya to kiss and ordered the nanny to tidy everything up, because the teacher was coming. He left.

The next day the doorbell rang.

The nanny ran out, returned, and began fussing.

"Your teacher has arrived, a face like an overgrown dog, you're in for it."

The teacher's heels clicked, she put her hand out to Katya. She really did look like a wise old watchdog, there were even some yellow spots around her eyes, and she turned her head so quickly and snapped her teeth, like she was catching a fly.

She looked over the nursery and said, "You're the nanny? Well then, if you would please gather all these toys and put them somewhere out of reach, so that the child doesn't see them. All of these donkeys and rams—clear them out! One must approach the toys logically and rationally, otherwise you'll have the disease of fantasy and the resulting damage. Katya, come over here."

She took a ball attached to a string out of her pocket and snapping her teeth, she began twirling the ball and humming: "Jump, skip, here, there, up and down, side and straight. Repeat after me: Jump, skip … Akh, what an underdeveloped child!"

Katya was quiet and smiled pitifully to keep from crying. The nanny carried away her toys, and the ram mewed in the doorway.

"Pay attention to the surface of this ball. What do you see? You see that it has two colors. One side is blue, the other white. Show me the blue side. You must try to focus."

She walked away, again stretching her hand out to Katya.

"Tomorrow we will weave baskets."

Katya trembled all evening and couldn't eat a thing. She kept thinking about her ram, but she was afraid to ask about him.

"It's terrible not to be alive. He can't do anything! He can't say a word, he can't call for me. And she said, 'Ou-t!'"

From that one terrible word, her entire soul ached and went cold.

The women came that evening, they ate, they whispered:

"So he says, so she says."

And again:

"Out! O-out!"

Katya woke up at dawn from horrible, unimaginable terror and longing. Somebody had been calling to her. She sat down, listened hard.

"Me-eh. Me-eh."

The ram was calling so pitiably, so mournfully, so desperately. The lifeless animal was crying.

She jumped off her bed; she was cold, her fists were balled up at her chest, she was listening. And again:

"Me-eh. Me-eh."

From somewhere in the hallway. He must be out there …

She opened the door.

"Me-eh."

From the storeroom.

She headed that way. It was unlocked. The dawn was turbid and dim, but already everything was visible. There were boxes, bundles.

"Me-eh. Me-eh."

Over by the window, there was a commotion of dark splotches, and there was the ram. Something dark jumped out, grabbed the ram by the head and was dragging it off.

"Me-eh. Me-eh."

And then two more, tearing at its sides, ripping its fleece.

"Rats! Rats!" Katya remembered Nanny's sharp teeth. She was trembling all over, clutched her fists even tighter. But he was no longer crying. He was no longer there. The plump rat had noiselessly dragged away the gray ribbons, the soft pieces, had torn apart the beast.

Katya hid in her bed, pulled the blanket over her head. She was silent and she didn't cry. She was afraid that Nanny would wake up, sneer like a cat, and laugh with the fox-like women at the woolly death of the lifeless animal.

She went completely quiet, squeezed herself as small as a nubbin. From now on she would live quietly, and nobody would ever know anything.

1916

MY LAST CHRISTMAS

Mikhail Zoshchenko

It's been a long time since I've celebrated Christmas.

The last time was about seven years ago.

Before Christmas itself I took a trip to some relatives in Petrograd. Luck wasn't on my side: I ended up having to spend the night at some rinky-dink station. The train was running twelve hours behind.

And the station really was rinky-dink. There wasn't even a buffet.

The security guard, by the way, was bragging: "In general, there's a buffet but nowsabout," on account of the holiday, it was closed. It was small comfort.

There were about twelve of us hapless travellers at this station. There was a fish merchant with a beard, two students, and some woman in an old-fashioned cloak, with two suitcases, and the others were folks unfamiliar to me.

Everybody sat submissively at the table in the tiny waiting hall and only the merchant showed signs of anger raging inside. He jumped up from the table, ran to the guard, and we could hear him squeal and puff himself up. One of the managers answered him calmly:

"There's no way of knowing … Eight in the morning … No earlier."

Among the passengers there was somebody else: a tidy-looking wee old man in a fur coat and a tall fur hat. At first the old man, laughing good-heartedly, comforted the passengers, gently looking in their eyes, then he took up singing in a quiet, reedy tenor: "Thy Birth, O Christ, Our Lord."

He was a wee old man with an absolutely pious appearance.

Good nature and meekness were visible in each of his movements.

He sat on a chair and, swaying in time, was singing "Thy Birth." But suddenly he popped up off the chair and disappeared from the station … A few minutes later he returned, holding in his hands a spruce twig.

"Here!" said the wee old man in exaltation, as we walked up to the table. "Here, dear ladies and gentlemen—behold we have a tree!"

And the wee old man proceeded to stick the tree in a decanter, humming softly, "Thy Birth, O Christ, Our Lord"

"Here, ladies and gentlemen," the old man said again, taking a few steps away from the table and admiring his handiwork, "On this festive day, because of somebody's sin, it is we who must sit here like the wretched of the earth …"

The passengers looked at the fussy figure of the little old man with displeasure and irritation.

"Yes," the old man continued, "because of somebody's sins … Of course, on this festive day, we—Orthodox Christians—are used to spending it amidst our friends and acquaintances. We are used to watching our little children jump in indescribable delight around the Christmas tree … Out of human weakness, fine ladies and gentlemen, we enjoy gobbling up ham with green peas and sausages one after another, and a slice of goose, and a tipple tipple of the you know what …"

"Tfu!" said the fishmonger, looking at the wee old man with disgust.

The passengers slid forward on their chairs.

"Yes, gentlefolk," the old man continued in the most delicate of tones, "we're used to spending this day in delight. However, even if that's not the case, you don't rail against God … They say, not far from here there's a small church, I'm going there … I'm going, fine gentlefolk, I'll cry my share of tears and light one of the wee candles …"

"Listen," said the merchant, "maybe we can get ahold of something? Perhaps we can get our hands on some, eh, some of that ham? Perhaps if you ask around?"

"I suspect it's possible," said the wee old man, "for money, dear ones, anything is possible. If we can get it together …"

The merchant extracted his wallet, banged it on the table, and began to count. The passengers happily turned in their seats, pulling out their bills.

In a few minutes, after counting the money they'd collected, the wee old man announced delightedly that there was enough for food and drink and more on top of that.

"Just don't be long," said the monger.

"I'll light a wee candle," said the old man, "cry a tear, ask the Orthodox Christians where I can make a purchase, and be back ... For whom among you, gentlefolk, shall I light a candle?"

"Light one for me," said the woman in the cloak, rummaging in her wallet and pulling out bills.

"No, Madame," said he, "allow me, with my most modest means, to do you a Christian deed. Who else among you?"

"In that case, for me," said the merchant, hiding his wallet.

The wee old man nodded his head and left. We could hear his voice: "Thy Birth, O Christ, Our Lord"

"What a saintly little old man," said the merchant.

"A surprising little old man," somebody seconded. And the passengers began to discuss the wee old man.

An hour went by. Then two. Then the clock struck five. The old man hadn't come. At seven o'clock in the morning he still wasn't there.

At seven thirty they signaled the train and the passengers rushed to grab a seat.

The train began to rumble.

It was still a bit dark. Suddenly it seemed to me that behind the corner of the station flashed the figure of the wee old man.

I rushed to the window. The old man concealed himself.

I exited onto the platform—and all of the sudden I distinctly heard the familiar reedy wee old tenor: "Thy Birth, O Christ, Our Lord"

That was my last Christmas.

Now I relate somewhat skeptically to religion.

1922

Anton Chekhov (1860-1904) was a practicing physician who wrote more than a dozen plays and two hundred short stories, among them the dramatic works *The Seagull* and *The Cherry Orchard*, and the story "Lady with a Lapdog." He is widely considered one of the greatest short story writers of all time and remains immensely popular in Russia and throughout the world.

Fyodor Dostoevsky (1821-1881) was the author of numerous novels, among them *Crime and Punishment* and *The Brothers Karamazov*, and short stories and novellas. An epileptic and gambler, Dostoevsky is perhaps most beloved for his portrayals of ethical dilemmas surrounding greed and beauty. As a young man, he belonged to a revolutionary terrorist organization and received a death sentence, which was later commuted to four years of hard labor in Siberia and compulsory military service.

Maxim Gorky (1868-1936), born Alexei Peshkov, was one of the first great writers of the Soviet Union and one of the founders of socialist realism. From 1906 to 1913, he lived on Capri in exile from the oppressive Tsarist regime, and from 1921-1928 he lived in mainland Italy, this time sheltering himself from an oppressive Communist government. His best known work is the novel *Mother*.

Vladimir Korolenko (1853-1921) was a Russian writer whose experience being exiled for revolutionary activities shaped his short stories and journalism. He traveled the globe and attended the 1893 Chicago World's Fair, and wrote the novel *Without Language* as a result of that trip—the first book, written in Russian, to deal with Russians in America.

Klaudia Lukashevich (1859-1931) was a children's author born in St. Petersburg into a family with Ukrainian roots. Her stories for children are mostly based on her own life. She was a teacher in Irkutsk, the Siberian city on Lake Baikal, and also worked for the Russian railroad after the death of her husband, which left her to care for her three children by herself.

Teffi (1872-1952) was the pseudonym of Nadezhda Buchinskaya née Lokhvitskaya. She was a humorist and mainstay of the satirical magazine *Satiricon*. She left Russia after the October Revolution of 1917, going first to Istanbul, then Paris, where she settled until the end of her life. Teffi was prolific and published many stories in émigré journals. Her best known short story collection is perhaps *The Witch*; she was also an accomplished memoirist.

Lev Tolstoy (1828-1910) was a prolific author and former soldier born to a noble family, best known for his novels *War and Peace* and *Anna Karenina*, his numerous short stories, and his religious meditations on life and death. His estate at Yasnaya Polyana became a place of pilgrimage for those seeking enlightenment and an audience with the great author.

Mikhail Zoshchenko (1894-1958) was one of the great Soviet satirists of the first half of the twentieth century. His collections of satirical short stories sold in the tens of millions in the USSR; he also wrote material for comic theaters. After World War II, his work was repressed by the Soviet government, and only toward the end of his life was he allowed to fully reenter the public sphere.

"A Christmas Tree and a Wedding,"
"At Christmastide,"
"A Woman's Kingdom,"
"The Little Boy at Christ's Christmas Tree"
translated by Constance Garnett

"The Boys"
translated by Marian Fell

"Makar's Dream"
translated by Suzanne Rosenberg

"Christmas Phantoms,"
"Dream of the Young Tsar"
translator unknown

"The New Year's Tree,"
"My Last Christmas,"
"A Distant Christmas Eve,"
"A Lifeless Animal"
translated by Ross Ufberg

***If Venice Dies* by Salvatore Settis**

Internationally renowned art historian Salvatore Settis ignites a new debate about the Pearl of the Adriatic and cultural patrimony at large. In this fiery blend of history and cultural analysis, Settis argues that "hit-and-run" visitors are turning Venice and other landmark urban settings into shopping malls and theme parks. This is a passionate plea to secure the soul of Venice, written with consummate authority, wide-ranging erudition and élan.

***The Madonna of Notre Dame* by Alexis Ragougneau**

Fifty thousand believers and photo-hungry tourists jam into Notre Dame Cathedral to celebrate the Feast of the Assumption. The next morning, a stunningly beautiful young woman kneels at prayer in a cathedral side chapel. But when an American tourist accidentally bumps against her, her body collapses. This thrilling murder mystery illuminates shadowy corners of the world's most famous cathedral, shedding light on good and evil with suspense, compassion and wry humor.

***Year of the Comet* by Sergei Lebedev**

From the critically acclaimed author of *Oblivion* comes *Year of the Comet*, a story of a Russian boyhood and coming of age as the Soviet Union is on the brink of collapse. Sergei Lebedev depicts a vast empire coming apart at the seams, transforming a very public moment into something tender and personal, and writes with shattering beauty and insight about childhood and the growing consciousness of a boy in the world.

***Moving the Palace* by Charif Majdalani**

A young Lebanese adventurer explores the wilds of Africa, encountering an eccentric English colonel in Sudan and enlisting in his service. In this lush chronicle of far-flung adventure, the military recruit crosses paths with a compatriot who has dismantled a sumptuous palace and is transporting it across the continent on a camel caravan. This is a captivating modern-day Odyssey in the tradition of Bruce Chatwin and Paul Theroux.

Adua by Igiaba Scego

Adua, an immigrant from Somalia to Italy, has lived in Rome for nearly forty years. She came seeking freedom from a strict father and an oppressive regime, but her dreams of film stardom ended in shame. Now that the civil war in Somalia is over, her homeland calls her. She must decide whether to return and reclaim her inheritance, but also how to take charge of her own story and build a future.

The 6:41 to Paris by Jean-Philippe Blondel

Cécile, a stylish 47-year-old, has spent the weekend visiting her parents outside Paris. By Monday morning, she's exhausted. These trips back home are stressful and she settles into a train compartment with an empty seat beside her. But it's soon occupied by a man she recognizes as Philippe Leduc, with whom she had a passionate affair that ended in her brutal humiliation 30 years ago. In the fraught hour and a half that ensues, Cécile and Philippe hurtle towards the French capital in a psychological thriller about the pain and promise of past romance.

On the Run with Mary by Jonathan Barrow

Shining moments of tender beauty punctuate this story of a youth on the run after escaping from an elite English boarding school. At London's Euston Station, the narrator meets a talking dachshund named Mary and together they're off on escapades through posh Mayfair streets and jaunts in a Rolls-Royce. But the youth soon realizes that the seemingly sweet dog is a handful; an alcoholic, nymphomaniac, drug-addicted mess who can't stay out of pubs or off the dance floor. *On the Run with Mary* mirrors the horrors and the joys of the terrible 20th century.

Oblivion by Sergei Lebedev

In one of the first 21st century Russian novels to probe the legacy of the Soviet prison camp system, a young man travels to the vast wastelands of the Far North to uncover the truth about a shadowy neighbor who saved his life, and whom he knows only as Grandfather II. Emerging from today's Russia, where the ills of the past are being forcefully erased from public memory, this masterful novel represents an epic literary attempt to rescue history from the brink of oblivion.

***The Last Weynfeldt* by Martin Suter**

Adrian Weynfeldt is an art expert in an international auction house, a bachelor in his mid-fifties living in a grand Zurich apartment filled with costly paintings and antiques. Always correct and well-mannered, he's given up on love until one night—entirely out of character for him—Weynfeldt decides to take home a ravishing but unaccountable young woman and gets embroiled in an art forgery scheme that threatens his buttoned up existence. This refined page-turner moves behind elegant bourgeois facades into darker recesses of the heart.

***The Last Supper* by Klaus Wivel**

Alarmed by the oppression of 7.5 million Christians in the Middle East, journalist Klaus Wivel traveled to Iraq, Lebanon, Egypt, and the Palestinian territories to learn about their fate. He found a minority under threat of death and humiliation, desperate in the face of rising Islamic extremism and without hope their situation will improve. An unsettling account of a severely beleaguered religious group living, so it seems, on borrowed time. Wivel asks, Why have we not done more to protect these people?

***Guys Like Me* by Dominique Fabre**

Dominique Fabre, born in Paris and a life-long resident of the city, exposes the shadowy, anonymous lives of many who inhabit the French capital. In this quiet, subdued tale, a middle-aged office worker, divorced and alienated from his only son, meets up with two childhood friends who are similarly adrift. He's looking for a second act to his mournful life, seeking the harbor of love and a true connection with his son. Set in palpably real Paris streets that feel miles away from the City of Light, a stirring novel of regret and absence, yet not without a glimmer of hope.

***Animal Internet* by Alexander Pschera**

Some 50,000 creatures around the globe—including whales, leopards, flamingoes, bats and snails—are being equipped with digital tracking devices. The data gathered and studied by major scientific institutes about their behavior will warn us about tsunamis, earthquakes and volcanic eruptions, but also radically transform our relationship to the natural world. Contrary to pessimistic fears, author Alexander Pschera sees the Internet as creating a historic opportunity for a new dialogue between man and nature.

Killing Auntie **by Andrzej Bursa**

A young university student named Jurek, with no particular ambitions or talents, finds himself with nothing to do. After his doting aunt asks the young man to perform a small chore, he decides to kill her for no good reason other than, perhaps, boredom. This short comedic masterpiece combines elements of Dostoevsky, Sartre, Kafka, and Heller, coming together to produce an unforgettable tale of murder and—just maybe—redemption.

I Called Him Necktie **by Milena Michiko Flašar**

Twenty-year-old Taguchi Hiro has spent the last two years of his life living as a hikikomori—a shut-in who never leaves his room and has no human interaction—in his parents' home in Tokyo. As Hiro tentatively decides to reenter the world, he spends his days observing life from a park bench. Gradually he makes friends with Ohara Tetsu, a salaryman who has lost his job. The two discover in their sadness a common bond. This beautiful novel is moving, unforgettable, and full of surprises.

Who is Martha? **by Marjana Gaponenko**

In this rollicking novel, 96-year-old ornithologist Luka Levadski foregoes treatment for lung cancer and moves from Ukraine to Vienna to make a grand exit in a luxury suite at the Hotel Imperial. He reflects on his past while indulging in Viennese cakes and savoring music in a gilded concert hall. Levadski was born in 1914, the same year that Martha—the last of the now-extinct passenger pigeons—died. Levadski himself has an acute sense of being the last of a species. This gloriously written tale mixes piquant wit with lofty musings about life, friendship, aging and death.

All Backs Were Turned **by Marek Hlasko**

Two desperate friends—on the edge of the law—travel to the southern Israeli city of Eilat to find work. There, Dov Ben Dov, the handsome native Israeli with a reputation for causing trouble, and Israel, his sidekick, stay with Ben Dov's younger brother, Little Dov, who has enough trouble of his own. Local toughs are encroaching on Little Dov's business, and he enlists his older brother to drive them away. It doesn't help that a beautiful German widow is rooming next door. A story of passion, deception, violence, and betrayal, conveyed in hard-boiled prose reminiscent of Hammett and Chandler.

Alexandrian Summer by Yitzhak Gormezano Goren

This is the story of two Jewish families living their frenzied last days in the doomed cosmopolitan social whirl of Alexandria just before fleeing Egypt for Israel in 1951. The conventions of the Egyptian upper-middle class are laid bare in this dazzling novel, which exposes sexual hypocrisies and portrays a vanished polyglot world of horse racing, seaside promenades and nightclubs.

Killing the Second Dog by Marek Hlasko

Two down-and-out Polish con men living in Israel in the 1950s scam an American widow visiting the country. Robert, who masterminds the scheme, and Jacob, who acts it out, are tough, desperate men, exiled from their native land and adrift in the hot, nasty underworld of Tel Aviv. Robert arranges for Jacob to run into the widow who has enough trouble with her young son to keep her occupied all day. What follows is a story of romance, deception, cruelty and shame. Hlasko's writing combines brutal realism with smoky, hard-boiled dialogue, in a bleak world where violence is the norm and love is often only an act.

Fanny von Arnstein: Daughter of the Enlightenment by Hilde Spiel

In 1776 Fanny von Arnstein, the daughter of the Jewish master of the royal mint in Berlin, came to Vienna as an 18-year-old bride. She married a financier to the Austro-Hungarian imperial court, and hosted an ever more splendid salon which attracted luminaries of the day. Spiel's elegantly written and carefully researched biography provides a vivid portrait of a passionate woman who advocated for the rights of Jews, and illuminates a central era in European cultural and social history.

The Missing Year of Juan Salvatierra by Pedro Mairal

At the age of nine, Juan Salvatierra became mute following a horse riding accident. At twenty, he began secretly painting a series of canvases on which he detailed six decades of life in his village on Argentina's frontier with Uruguay. After his death, his sons return to deal with their inheritance: a shed packed with rolls over two miles long. But an essential roll is missing. A search ensues that illuminates links between art and life, with past family secrets casting their shadows on the present.

***Cocaine* by Pitigrilli**

Paris in the 1920s—dizzy and decadent. Where a young man can make a fortune with his wits ... unless he is led into temptation. Cocaine's dandified hero Tito Arnaudi invents lurid scandals and gruesome deaths, and sells these stories to the newspapers. But his own life becomes even more outrageous when he acquires three demanding mistresses. Elegant, witty and wicked, Pitigrilli's classic novel was first published in Italian in 1921 and retains its venom even today.

***The Good Life Elsewhere* by Vladimir Lorchenkov**

The very funny—and very sad—story of a group of villagers and their tragicomic efforts to emigrate from Europe's most impoverished nation to Italy for work. An Orthodox priest is deserted by his wife for an art-dealing atheist; a mechanic redesigns his tractor for travel by air and sea; and thousands of villagers take to the road on a modern-day religious crusade to make it to the Italian Promised Land. A country where 25 percent of its population works abroad, remittances make up nearly 40 percent of GDP, and alcohol consumption per capita is the world's highest – Moldova surely has its problems. But, as Lorchenkov vividly shows, it's also a country whose residents don't give up easily.

***Some Day* by Shemi Zarhin**

On the shores of Israel's Sea of Galilee lies the city of Tiberias, a place bursting with sexuality and longing for love. The air is saturated with smells of cooking and passion. *Some Day* is a gripping family saga, a sensual and emotional feast that plays out over decades. This is an enchanting tale about tragic fates that disrupt families and break our hearts. Zarhin's hypnotic writing renders a painfully delicious vision of individual lives behind Israel's larger national story.

To purchase these titles and for more information please visit newvesselpress.com.

New Vessel Press is committed to preserving ancient forests and natural resources. We elected to print this title on 30% postconsumer recycled paper, processed chlorine-free. As a result, for this printing, we have saved:

6 Trees (40' tall and 6-8" diameter)
3 Million BTUs of Total Energy
510 Pounds of Greenhouse Gases
2,763 Gallons of Wastewater
185 Pounds of Solid Waste

New Vessel Press made this paper choice because our printer, Thomson-Shore, Inc., is a member of Green Press Initiative, a nonprofit program dedicated to supporting authors, publishers, and suppliers in their efforts to reduce their use of fiber obtained from endangered forests.

For more information, visit www.greenpressinitiative.org

Environmental impact estimates were made using the Environmental Defense Paper Calculator. For more information visit: www.edf.org/papercalculator